the

Witches

of

BlackBrook

by

Tish Thawer

Amber Leaf Publishing
Divide, Colorado

First Edition
First Printing, 2015
ISBN: 978-0692457948
Library of Congress Control Number: 2015909556

Cover design by Regina Wamba of Mae I Design and Photography
Edited by Laura Bruzan

This is a work of fiction. Names, characters, places, organizations,
and events portrayed in this novel are either products of the author's
imagination or are used fictitiously. And any resemblance to actual
persons (living or dead), business establishments, or locales is entirely
coincidental. Any brand names have been used under the Fair Use
Act.

Amber Leaf Publishing, Divide, Colorado
www.amberleafpublishing.com
www.tishthawer.com

Praise for *Scent of a White Rose*

"Thawer managed what I thought was an impossible feat. She was able to put yet another new spin on the age old vampire tale." ~ *The Bookshelf Sophisticate*

"...everything about *Scent of a White Rose* was such a fresh new concept when it came to vampires, actually it was just a whole new concept in general for the paranormal genre! This is a read any paranormal lover should read!" ~ *YA-Aholic*

"*Scent of a White Rose* is not the plain Jane girl meets vampire and falls in love story...I will tell you that you should add this book to your TBR list." ~ *The Book Nympho*

"Tish Thawer crafts a seductive vampire tale with her eloquent writing style and keen sense of romance that simply entrances." ~ *Romancing the Darkside*

"Sensual, passionate, and thrilling, describes "Scent of a White Rose". This unique, beautifully descriptive, and highly imaginative plotline is full of kick-ass twists, and the concept of "drifting" in which the feelings of vampires are visible through the changing colors of their hair, eyes and skin at different stages of their emotions, tickled me pink. ~ *Goodreads Reviewer*

Praise for *Aradia Awakens*

"Tish Thawer is one of those authors whose works are marked by something incredibly special. With each book she writes, I am awed by the magickal elements in each novel." ~ *Author Rae Hachton*

"The author skillfully weaves a tale so intense that you can't help but want more." ~ *The Cover and Everything in Between*

"Once more, I was overwhelmed by the creativity and imagination that comes from this author..." ~ *Proserpine Craving Books*

"I really, really like the world of Ovialell. The world is unique, complex, and full of all sorts of paranormal species. There are werewolves, vampires, amazons, Goddesses, there are so many interesting elements to the world." ~ *The Book Savvy Babe*

"A wonderful brew of Goddess's, and shifters, vampires, Amazonians, and even the Fae. Tish had me completely engaged in this novel to the point that I could not put it down. I adore the main characters of Aryiah and Damarius. Aryiah is a kick ass heroine and Damarius is a perfect alpha male lead. He is smoking hot and sexy as all get out, add being a wolf to that and just WOW. 5 Stars for Tish Thawer!" ~ *Author & Reader Con*

Praise for *Raven's Breath*

" ...this was an addicting, thrill ride of a read which kept me turning pages and cursing real life that kept interrupting me... A new take on a tale that is literally as old as time, I would challenge anyone to predict the ending. Brilliant!" ~ *NerdGirl*

"The plot is wonderful. The characters are amazing and fun. Tish Thawer's Raven's Breath is unique story. Meet the only female Grim Reaper...There are so many thing that I love about this book but my favorite is the twist at the end." ~ *GoodReads Reviewer*

"...I now rate this story as one of my all-time faves. Raven is the first female Grim Reaper. One would think that would make for a dark, sinister story line. Well, it does, but not in the way you'd think. Ms. Thawer also breathes humor, light, and romance into this Sci-Fi novel. I love Raven's character, with her spunkiness, gumption, and self-deprecating humor. The scenes are lushly drawn, and the other characters grab your interest and add so much to an already wonderful story. If you've never read Sci-Fi before, read this as your first. If you love a great plot, read this. If you haven't finished it by Sunday evening, call in sick to work Monday morning. You'll be glad you did. I am so looking forward to reading the next in this series!" ~ *Amazon Reviewer*

Also by Tish Thawer

The Rose Trilogy

Scent of a White Rose – Book 1

Roses & Thorns – Book 1.5

Blood of a Red Rose – Book 2

Death of a Black Rose – Book 3

Aradia Awakens - Book 1

Prophecy's Child - Companion

The Rise of Rae - Companion

Shay and the Box of Nye - Companion

Behind the Veil - Omnibus

The Women of Purgatory

Raven's Breath - Book 1

Dark Abigail - Book 2

Acknowledgements

To all who inspire me with your art, your words, your loyalty, and support. Thank you.

To my family, by blood or by spirit, you are my constant source of inspiration. I love you.

"We are the granddaughters of the witches you weren't able to burn."

— Unknown

the

Witches

of

BlackBrook

Prologue

IPSWICH, MASSACHUSETTS
1693

Flames licked the hem of her dress as she worked to free her hands from the ropes. Somber faces, etched with malice or fear, looked on as she squirmed against the stake. She refused to close her eyes or scream. She wouldn't give them that. No. She would prove to be as defiant and wild as they deemed her while dragging her from her home.

Kara and Kenna stood hidden at the back of the crowd, silently pleading for her to use magic to escape. She wanted to, oh how she wanted to, just to see these *Puritans* running for the hills. But, staring into her sister's eyes as her legs started to burn, she knew she had to do whatever it took to keep them safe.

She closed her eyes, the chant beginning simple as always, words from the Goddess flowing into her mind. *"Come to me, death that be, flames surrounds, peace abounds; flesh to earth, spirit to soar, transport our souls, alive forever more."*

Chapter One

BLACKBROOK, NY

Present Day

She pulled the fur of her hood around her face as the wind whipped against her skin. New York was her home and had been for the entire twenty-five years of this particular lifetime, so you'd think she'd be used to the harsh winters by now. *Freezing my face off? Not sure I'll ever get used to this,* Trin thought to herself.

With a hand-held shovel she approached her car, hidden from sight under a glittering blanket of white, and sighed. Four minutes in and she was wishing she could use her magic or that

3

she could at least hail a cab. Unfortunately, until she found her other sister, her small pool of magic wasn't going to be sending her anywhere fast. As for the taxi, BlackBrook was a small northern town in upstate New York, one that practically shut down once a snowstorm hit. Trin kicked the drift firmly set against her tire, cursing the fact she was probably one of only a handful of people who had to go to work on this frigid day.

Five minutes later with barely any progress made, Trin spotted a police car creeping down her icy street. Stepping around the hood of her Volvo, she waved her arms in the symbolic *"Come help me"* gesture.

"Morning." The handsome officer smiled. "Need a lift?"

The idea of putting her life in someone else's hands in these conditions was terrifying, but there was no denying she wouldn't make it to work on time if she continued to dig out her own ride. "Yes, please. BlackBrook Wellness Center if you don't mind."

"I don't mind at all. Hop in."

Trin climbed into the front seat of the squad car, depositing her wet shovel onto the floor between her feet.

"Thank you so much."

"It's no problem, I'm here to serve." He glanced in her direction, a small smile playing at the corner of his lips. "I'm Officer Hardy."

Officer Hardy, or Jason she'd found out from the girls at

work, was the newest transplant to BlackBrook, accompanied only by his cousin, Caris, a kindergarten teacher at the local private school who Trin had yet to meet. Apparently, though, they shared bright hazel eyes, and from what Trin had been told, kind hearts the pair of them.

"It's nice to meet you. How are you and your cousin enjoying BlackBrook?"

"It's great, thank you."

Trin rubbed her gloved hands in front of the heater vents. "Are you both used to working in this kind of weather?" Trin asked.

"Yes, but Caris has a snow-day today and I suspect she'll spend most of it asleep—Or not."

Trin looked up to see an unfamiliar Jeep parked outside the Wellness Center and quickly made the connection. Jason parked next to his cousin's ride, exited the car, and followed Trin into the building.

The interior of the local spa was calming and serene with smooth mahogany and sea-colored glass throughout. Soft instrumentals played non-stop, and fragrant oils permeated the air. Trin bid Officer Hardy a good day, then waved at Mia, the receptionist, on her way to the back room. Lifting the latch on her assigned locker, Trin deposited her belongings then returned to the front desk, anxious to retrieve the file for her first client of the day.

Caris Hardy, New Member

Occupation: Teacher

Preferred Pressure: Medium to Deep

Problem Areas: Upper back, lower back, shoulder blades, and neck.

Trin laughed internally. Caris may not be sleeping on her day off yet, but after a relaxing massage, a little R&R was definitely in her near future.

"Caris?" Trin whispered as she peeked into the waiting area.

Caris Hardy looked more like a college student than a teacher. She was nestled into one of the comfy leather chairs next to the fireplace with her auburn hair piled high, wearing sweatpants, boots, and a flannel button-down under her long winter coat. Upon hearing her name, she opened her bright eyes and smiled kindly.

"Good morning, Ms. Hardy. Are you ready for your massage?" Trin asked.

"Oh, you have no idea." Caris beamed.

Trin led her new client down the hall, turning towards the furthest room at the end. "Here we are." Trin gestured with a wave of her hand then followed Caris inside. "So, what are we doing today? Full-body, or are there specific problem areas you'd like me to focus on?"

"If we could focus on the upper body, that would be great.

As you'll see, I hold a lot of tension in my neck and shoulder blades."

"Of course, no problem. Please undress to your comfort level and we'll start face-down. I'll give you a few minutes," Trin explained.

"Okay, thanks."

Trin shut the door, giving Ms. Hardy the allotted two minutes to get settled, then knocked quietly and reentered. "All set?"

"Yes, come on in."

Trin dimmed the lights and checked the bed-warmer, then set Caris's file onto the cabinet counter before turning to face the table. Her practiced ritual of lowering and refolding the sheets and blankets down her client's back was interrupted with another internal giggle. The petite Ms. Hardy was covered in tattoos.

Trin wasn't one to judge, having tattoos herself, but the dichotomy of what this person did versus who she really was, had her amused. Trin found herself truly interested in getting to know more about this woman.

"Your tattoos are beautiful," Trin said as she adjusted the bolster.

"Thank you," came Caris's quick reply.

Trin dispensed her homemade lotion into her hands and reached for Caris's shoulders.

"Ouch!" Trin exclaimed, pulling back her hand.

"Oh my god, what was that?" Caris lifted her head.

"I'm not sure. There usually isn't any static build-up in the rooms, but boy, that was one heck of a shock. I'm so sorry."

"It's okay. Must be my electric personality," Caris joked.

Trin laughed nervously and rubbed her hands together once more. "I'd buy that."

Caris lowered her head back into the cradle and Trin began again, this time with no surprises.

Much to Trin's dismay, the hour flew by. She and Caris had talked more about her tattoos, her move and new job in BlackBrook, and of course, her cousin, who turned out to be single.

Trin handed Ms. Hardy a glass of water as she walked out of the room.

"Thanks, again, Trin. This was heaven. I will definitely be back to see you soon."

"I'd love that. Also, remember to drink lots of water, and a warm bath with some Epsom salt wouldn't be a bad idea either."

"You got it," Caris replied.

Trin gave a final wave as Caris left the building, then went to clear and turn the room. After refreshing the sheets and resetting the table, she took an extra minute to glance at Ms. Hardy's file. There wasn't much information beyond the basics:

address, occupation, emergency contact, etc. Trin returned the file to the cabinet behind the front desk and glanced at her watch.

"Mia, I'm gonna take my break now. I'll be back in a few."

The blonde receptionist nodded her head and continued talking into her headpiece.

Trin entered the locker room and grabbed her cell phone from her purse, holding down the number two.

"Kit, I think I've found her!"

Chapter Two

"I'm telling you, I think it's her. I'll fill you in when I get home." Trin huffed. "Actually, will you be able to pick me up? I caught a ride to work this morning and now I'm stranded." Trin pouted. "Okay, great. Thanks. See ya later."

Trin returned her cell to her locker and closed the door. She had four more clients today and was looking forward to the tips from each one. Tonight would require a celebration, so she'd have Kit stop on their way home and buy some wine.

Trin greeted her next client and went through her practiced motions, losing herself over the next hour-and-a-half to the memories of a time when all three sisters had still been a family.

IPSWICH, MASSACHUSETTS
1683

"Karina, Kara, Kenna, gather 'round."

The girls tucked their dark red locks under the hood of their woolen cloaks and took their positions at their mother's side. This was the first time they all three would be participating in an Esbat together, with little Kenna just turning six.

"All right, Kara, take this censer in your hand. Kenna, you hold the bowl of water. Karina, you'll cast the circle, then make the callings with your wand."

Karina nodded and removed her wand from the pocket of her cloak, then stepped to the easternmost point of their circle and began. "I cast this circle, once around, all within, magic bound. Protected from harm and sealed this night, through the Goddess's energy the charm's alight."

Kenna reached out to the stump where all their tools precisely lay and added a pinch of salt to the bowl of water like she'd seen her mother do time and time again. Then, pacing the circle, she followed Karina's steps, sprinkling the contents as she went. "I cast this circle, twice around, all within, magic bound. Cleansed with water, strengthened with earth, sealed this night with Spirit's mirth." Kenna returned the bowl to the altar and received a reassuring nod from her mother as she stood again in her place.

Next, Kara lit the sage and cedar within the censer and lifted the feather from its position on the left side of the altar, then encircled the space. "I cast this circle, thrice around, all within, magic bound. Inspired by air and sealed this night, protected from harm by Spirit's might." Kara returned the burner and feather to the altar, her protection set in place.

Karina moved back to the easternmost point, ready to make the callings. "Spirits of Air, hear my call. Protect this rite from one and all." The pentacle she drew in the air glowed yellow in response.

Turning south she repeated the process. "Spirits of Fire, hear my call. Protect this rite from one and all." The pentacle glowed red like the flames of a fire. She glanced at her mama and received an encouraging smile.

Turning west she continued. "Spirits of Water, hear my call. Protect this rite from one and all." This was her favorite. The bright blue pentacle sparked and danced from the end of her wand.

Turning north she completed the callings. "Spirits of Earth, hear my call. Protect this rite from one and all." The final pentacle shown bright green like the lush forest in which they stood.

"Well done, girls, simple and exactly enough." Their mother then anointed two candles, one silver and one gold, placing each into a homemade wooden holder lined with lavender snips. "Lord and Lady, we invoke thee. Join us now for this sacred rite, protecting us with your love and might. Guide us now, in all we do, blessing our path, forged straight and true. Hail and welcome." Flames burst to life, bathing their circle with an ethereal glow. "Girls, please come forward and deposit a single strand of your hair into the cauldron."

Karina, Kara, and Kenna each did so in turn, receiving their mother's kiss upon completion.

"Goddess of love, Goddess of light, bless my girls on this full moon's night. Spark their powers from deep within, let their journey as witches begin."

A hot white light burst from the cauldron, spanning the circle and passing straight through the girls.

"My beautiful daughters. Your path has officially begun. Take all I've taught you and let the Goddess now guide you, for you will be more powerful than I could have ever hoped. Together remain, and from fighting refrain, as the bond you share, time will not wear. So mote it be."

"So mote it be," the girls intoned in unison.

Beep, beep, beep. Trin's timer yanked her swiftly from the past.

"All right, Mr. Pruitt, that concludes our session for today."

Trin moved through the rest of her appointments much the same, drifting through memories with a refreshed sense of hopefulness that her sister witch would finally be coming home.

After folding the sheets and clearing her room for the last time, Trin grabbed her things from her locker and checked her phone to confirm her ride.

Kit: *Trin, looks like I can't pick you up after all, sorry. Can you get a different ride?*

Trin shot back her reply.

Trin: *Not sure. I'll let you know. :)*

Damn, Trin cursed. Who could she call in this weather to ask for a lift? Her mind supplied the answer immediately and after a quick search on her phone, she dialed the number for the local police station.

"Hello, could I please speak to Officer Hardy?...Trin Hartwell....Thank you."

Trin stood, smiling to herself as she recalled Jason's earlier words, *"I'm here to serve."*

"Hello? Trin? Is everything all right?"

"Hi, Officer Hardy. Yes, everything is fine. It's just that by flagging you down this morning, I've left myself in a bit of a pickle. I need a ride home and wondered if you'd be willing to repeat the kind gesture?"

"Of course, it would be my pleasure. I'll see you in ten."

Trin exhaled. "Great! Thanks so much." She started to ask if they could make a pit stop for wine but thought the request inappropriate and halted her words. She didn't want to give Jason the wrong impression of her. Then again, why would it matter? It wasn't as if she had any hopes of starting a relationship with him—not that she wanted to. If Caris *was* in fact Kara reincarnated, then through whatever twist of fate that brought them into this time, Jason and her must somehow be related through their distant past. So yeah...there goes that idea.

What idea? Why are you even thinking about this? Trin shook her head and gathered her things, making her way to the front door to await her non-relationship-material ride to show up.

Eight minutes later she was once again cozy in the front seat of a cop car, feeling completely awkward for the first time in a very long time.

"So, were you able to fix my cousin?" Officer Hardy joked.

"I hope so," Trin smiled.

A beep on her phone drew her attention. It was another message from Kit.

Kit: *Did you manage a ride?*

Trin stole a look at Jason.

Trin: *Yes. When will you be home?*

Kit: *2 days. Heading to NYC now. Show got bumped up.*

Trin huffed. Kit was an artist, a good artist who had several showings in Manhattan on a reoccurring basis. Her upcoming event had been planned for next week, and in light of Trin's experience today and her pending celebration tonight, the change in schedule couldn't have come at a worse time.

Trin: *Okay. Fill you in once you're back. Be safe.*

Kit: *You too.*

"Something wrong?" Jason asked.

Kit noticed the police car had come to a stop, but it wasn't in front of her house. Instead, she found herself outside the local strip mall and cast a speculative glance at Officer Hardy.

"What are we doing here?"

"I asked first."

"What?"

"I asked you a question first. Is something wrong? You answer me, then I'll answer you." Jason's confident air pricked at her, but his adorable smile, broad shoulders, chestnut hair, and hazel eyes had a way of putting her at ease.

Trin shook her head. "No. Nothing's wrong. My roommate had to leave town, and I was hoping to have dinner with her to discuss something important. Now it'll have to wait, that's all."

"Can't you call her later?"

"Not really. This has to be discussed in person." Trin crinkled her nose.

"Okay, my turn. We are here because I'm officially off duty and was going to ask if you'd like to join me for dinner." Jason gestured to the Italian restaurant directly in front of them. "Caris has informed me that after the amazing massage she received today, she would be relaxing for the rest of the evening and not cooking."

Trin laughed. "Oh my. Maybe I should pay to cover your inconvenience?"

Jason squinted and dropped his smile. "Ms. Hartwell, I'm not sure what you're used to, but I'd never let a woman I've invited to dinner foot the bill."

Trin caught the false seriousness of his tone and knew that while he meant what he said, he wasn't actually offended. "From your tone and words, you sound as if you're asking me out." *What the hell am I doing?*

"Now you're catching on." Jason winked and flashed his dazzling smile once more.

Shit. "All right, Mr. Hardy, you've got yourself a date."

Chapter Three

Blood dripped into the charred stone bowl. "Block her sight, dark as night, separate must she be. Take this blood, and break this bond, never again the three." A high-pitched screech filled the cave as drops of crimson dripped from his wrist and into the stone cauldron. He spat onto the sizzling potion, infuriated the time had come again for him to pretend to be something he wasn't. Witch's spells, though while they worked for him, always burnt his tongue.

Trin and Jason made their way into *Milano North*, exchanging small talk while they waited for a table. It was the only Italian restaurant in BlackBrook and was busy even on the coldest of nights.

"So, how long have you been working at the spa," Jason asked as they finally slid into a booth at the back.

"About five years. I went straight to massage therapy school out of high school, and was hired at the Wellness Center upon my graduation."

"That's great. Not a lot of people know what they want to do right out of school," Jason smiled.

"Didn't you? I mean, have you not always been a cop?"

"Oh, no. I have. Straight to the academy, but in general, I think a lot of kids these days don't have a clue where they see themselves in a month, let alone five to twenty years from now."

"That's so true. But I've always known I wanted to help people. I thought about becoming a doctor, but didn't want to wait twelve or more years before I could feel like I was making a difference." Trin shrugged. "A lot of people don't get it, but massage can really help someone in a lot of ways." Trin didn't mention the magical touch she used during her sessions. She was a healer and skin-to-skin contact was one of the ways her magic worked.

Jason stared at Trin with a tilt to his head. "You're interesting, Trin. I like you."

"Such a bold statement for someone who's just met me," she teased.

"I may have just met you, but I feel like I've known you forever." Jason winked as he reached across the table, taking her hand. A blue spark flared at the point of contact. "Whoa. What was that?"

"My electric personality?" Trin giggled, amused at using his cousin's earlier words, then stopped short. She had to stop flirting with him if Caris was who she thought she was.

Trin straightened, pulling back her hand. "Jason, look. You seem really nice, and I'm so very grateful for your help today and for dinner, but I don't want to lead you on. I can't follow this to any conclusion you might be expecting, and I think it's best if I tell you that now."

A slow smirk crept across Jason's face. "Well, Ms. Hartwell, aren't we full of ourselves? I simply stated that I found you interesting and that I liked you. That doesn't mean I'm looking for a relationship."

Trin was mortified. How could she have read things so inaccurately?

"I'm a man of few words, Trin, so I don't like to mince them. I truly do feel as if I've known you forever, and I'd like to spend more time with you because I enjoy your company. If

I start to feel anything more, you'll be the first to know."

"I'm sorry, Jason. I just..." Trin stuttered.

"Don't apologize. Being single these days can be a difficult thing to navigate. That's why I like you, though, you put me at ease and seem so...real."

"Well, thank you. I do try to stay grounded and centered, though with this ridiculous display, I have failed miserably." Trin laughed, feeling lighter again.

"No harm, no foul. Are you ready to order?"

"Yes, thank you."

Trin and Jason gave the waitress their order and continued their evening, relaxed and engaged. By the time Officer Hardy dropped her off outside her house, Trin shared his earlier sentiment. "Jason, tonight's been great. Thank you again, and you're right, it does feel like I've known you forever. Give me a call anytime, and be sure to tell Caris hello for me as well, I hope to see her again soon."

"How about you come over to our place tomorrow? It's the first Saturday we've both had off together in ages. We plan to cook, watch movies, and hang out. You're more than welcome to join us."

"Oh, wow. Thanks. That does sound great, but I wouldn't want to intrude on your joint day off."

"Nonsense. Please come." Jason flashed a confident smile and Trin felt her resolve slipping once more.

"Okay. Sounds fun. Anything I can bring?"

"Just the wine." Jason winked.

They exchanged numbers, then Trin exited the cruiser and unlocked her front door, waving goodbye from her stoop before stepping inside.

"Who was that?"

Trin screamed, spinning to find Kit sitting on the couch.

"Jesus. You scared the crap out of me. What are you doing here? I thought you were on your way to the city?"

"I was, but Harold called shortly after I got on the road. They moved the show back again. Another ice storm." Kit shrugged.

Trin hung her purse on one arm of the coat stand, depositing her jacket onto another. "Well, I'm glad your home, because I can't wait to tell you what happened today."

"Do we need wine?" Kit lifted her eyebrows.

"Sorry, I wasn't able to stop for any."

Kit unfolded her legs and jumped off the couch. "I was!"

Trin laughed, tossing flames from her fingertips, setting the fire alight. She followed Kit into the kitchen and grabbed two glasses from the cabinet.

"Okay, well, today, my first client was the new teacher in town, Caris Hardy."

"Wait, wait, wait. Back up. How did you get to work and how does the cute guy fit in?"

"Oh, yeah. Jason...he's the officer who gave me a ride to work this morning. I didn't have time to dig out my car. And, *Officer Hardy* is Caris's cousin."

"Oohhh, how very entwined," Kit grinned.

"Indeed. Anyway. When I first touched Caris there was a massive shock between us. I blew it off of course, but in reality, as I massaged across her tattoos I was flooded with visions. Visions of us in the past. All three of us."

Kit's eyes dropped to the glass in her hand. "Really? You're sure it was us?"

"I'm sure. I was once again Karina and was there with you and Kara. It was us. Our original selves."

Kit sighed then with a gentle smile laid a hand on Trin's shoulder. "Trin, you know as well as I do that that doesn't mean it's her. In our last life, you had a similar vision and it was because your spirit recognized the energy of another witch. It wasn't Kara then and I doubt it is now."

Trin dropped her head, crestfallen as she always was when Kit brought her back to reality—a feat her little sister performed all too often.

"I'm sorry, Katrine. I just don't want you to get your hopes up again, then spend another year depressed when your hunch proves to be wrong." Kit's tone was soft and gentle, but did nothing to ease Trin's disappointment.

"Perhaps you're right. I doubt our reincarnated sister

would spontaneously show up with a cousin this time. It was always just us three, and I know it will be again." Trin shook her head, mentally discarding her theory.

"We'll keep looking. I promise. You and I are always able to find each other in whatever life we live, and soon, I know we'll be able to find Kara too," Kit promised.

"Okay. Maybe we could do another scrying spell on the next full moon."

"Yes. Let's. But for now, how about we enjoy our wine in front of the TV and the cozy fire you've created?"

Trin smiled. "Sounds great. Speaking of the wine, this is good." She lifted her glass for another sip. "Where did you get it?"

"*Lost in Time*, a little specialty place outside of town on the 9N."

"Ironic, and perfect. I'll be able to grab a bottle on my way to the Hardy's tomorrow."

Kit's glass shattered in her hand.

Trin jumped. "Jesus! Are you okay?"

Kit shook her hand out over the sink, taking a deep breath. "Yes, I'm fine," she stated, wrapping a towel around the thin stream of blood running down the side of her palm.

Trin cleaned up the wine and broken shards littering the floor, then looked up to find Kit watching her like a hawk.

"What?"

"Nothing. I'm sorry I've ruined our night. I'm going to go tend to this then head to bed."

"Just let me," Trin said as she reached for Kit's bleeding hand.

Kit pulled away. "You know I can heal myself. I don't need your help."

Trin frowned and crossed her arms. *What the hell is wrong with her?* Kit had always been somewhat petulant and stubborn, but lately, she was bordering on downright rude. Leaving her be, Trin eased onto the couch and watched the fire dance as she enjoyed the rest of her wine. Her mind wandered back to a time when she was able to use her healing gifts freely within their home.

IPSWICH, MASSACHUSETTS
1686

"Karina, keep close watch on your sisters while I'm gone. I should be back before day's end."

"Yes, Mama."

"Girls, if you're good for Karina I may have a surprise for you when I return."

Kara and Kenna squealed with excitement and started running around the kitchen, sweeping and cleaning to prove their worth. They obviously wanted their surprise.

With the house tidy and the worsh hung on the line, Karina settled the girls at the table and dug out their spellbooks. Now that they had been blessed as witches, their mother encouraged them each to create their own book of shadows, as it was meant to be.

"Let's work on a spell that gets rid of all the dust in the house," little Kenna suggested.

"No, Kenna. You cannot use magic to take away your chores. Sweeping and dusting are tasks that ground you to this world. Be grateful you have a home to clean."

Kenna smiled and nodded at her big sister's wise words.

"We could work on controlling water, since we've already mastered fire," Kara offered.

"Yes, we could, for that is an important skill. Why don't you two gather the scrying bowl and start with that," Karina instructed.

"What are you going to do?" Kara asked.

"I feel the need to hone my healing skills this day."

Karina moved to their work area in the back room next to the kitchen and began to pull herbs from the cabinet. Arrowroot for cleansing, healing, and purification, birch shavings to remove negative energy and hexes, and evening primrose for healing and protection. Using the pestle and mortar she ground the herbs, setting them to steep over the fire then passed a beeswax candle through the vapor being produced. Setting her ingredients aside, she put ink to her book and notated the spell that was flowing into her mind.

Illness from an unnatural place, be gone from this person, leave in grace. Cleansed and healed you are anew, blessed by the Goddess, through and through.

As Karina returned the ink and quill back to the work cabinet, Kara and Kenna gasped.

"What is it?" Karina asked.

"Mama. There's something wrong with Mama," Kara exclaimed as Kenna started to cry.

Just then the door flew open and their mother struggled to cross the threshold, collapsing as she did.

"Mama!" Karina exclaimed.

Karina and Kara helped their mother into the parlor, while Kenna gathered the spilled items from her basket.

"What's wrong with her?" Kara begged.

"I'm not sure yet. Give me room." Karina took a deep breath, then placed her hands on her mother's head and heart. Drawing on her magic, Karina focused within her mother and felt a deep seeded wrongness. Whatever was causing their mother to be in this state, was not natural.

"Kara, quick, gather a cup of the herbs I have on the fire. Kenna, bring me my book of shadows."

The girls moved at lightning speed. Returning the requested objects in seconds.

Karina lifted their mother's head and slowly poured drops of the herbal concoction past her lips. Handing the cup back to Kara, she then quickly grabbed her book from Kenna's shaking hands.

"Illness from an unnatural place, be gone from this person, leave in grace. Cleansed and healed you are anew, blessed by the Goddess, through and through." Karina repeated the spell she'd written only minutes ago.

A deep careening sigh escaped their mother as if she herself were a tea kettle set to steep. The girls stood back, held hands, and waited.

Karina rushed back to her mother's side when her eyes fluttered open.

"You've done well, my child. You're a strong healer, Karina. And girls," she reached for Kara and Kenna, "your powers of foresight have proven keen as well. I'm so proud of you all."

Chapter Four

Trin woke to the sound of sizzling bacon and percolating coffee.

"Good morning, sleepy head," Kit teased.

"Morning." Trin looked around the living room, noticing her empty wine glass and a discarded blanket lying on the floor. "Must have fallen asleep on the couch," she mumbled.

"Obviously." Kit laughed. "How much of that wine did you end up drinking?"

"Just the one glass." Trin shook her head, attempting to shake the strange grogginess she was experiencing.

"Well, hopefully you got a good night's sleep, because today, we're going shopping."

"Wait. What? I told you I have plans this afternoon." Trin rubbed her eyes and she poured her first cup of coffee. And yes, there would be multiple.

Kit scowled as she turned back to the stove. "Oh, that's right."

Trin took a seat at the bar and sipped her coffee as she watched Kit work. Her auburn hair was pulled up in its usual high ponytail, and her tan complexion was sprinkled with freckles, just like Trin's. "What is wrong with you? The first time I mentioned going to the Hardy's you bust a wine glass in your hand, and now you look downright pissed. What gives?"

Kit forked the bacon onto a plate and set it in front of Trin with a sigh.

"I just don't want you to get hurt. I think the more time you spend with them, the more ways you'll try to justify that Caris is, in fact, Kara, and I'm not ready to pick up the pieces again."

An image of herself crying into Kit's arms flashed into Trin's mind. Uncertain if she, or Kit, projected it there, she clenched her jaw and kept her mouth shut. Kit may be right, but she wasn't going to change her plans because of it.

"Look. Go. Have fun with your new friends, but keep in mind that that's all they can be. Caris can't possibly be Kara if she has a male cousin. Soul travel doesn't work that way. I've shown up as your friend, stranger, roommate, etc. over multiple lifetimes, but it's always been just me—a single female until we found one another and our power sparked. Regardless of our outward circumstances, it's then that we become true sisters again."

Trin took a bite of the bacon and smiled. "Don't worry, sis. I'll be fine."

Kit left the kitchen without another word, leaving Trin to plan her day in peace. She glanced at the clock—10:30am. First, a shower, obviously, then a trip to the market was in order.

Trin dressed in jeans and boots, then layered a thick cream cable knit sweater over her tank top. Donning her fur-lined jean jacket, she settled her long auburn hair in place with a cream beanie.

Digging out her car proved less difficult now that the sun had rose to its mid-point in the sky. The snow was still thick on the ground, but the warm rays not only thawed the ice, but also brightened her mood. Trin pulled her Volvo into the grocery store parking lot a little after one o'clock, excited to gather the items on her list.

While Jason had indicated all she needed to bring was the wine, Trin couldn't in good conscience arrive with nothing to contribute to the meal. She gathered fresh sweet and yellow potatoes, some course sea salt and black pepper, and a small jar of extra virgin olive oil. Stopping next at *Lost in Time*, she picked up two bottles of the sweet moscato she'd enjoyed last night.

Jason's text came through around three o'clock, supplying their address and indicating that she could head over whenever she liked. Trin fired up her GPS and began to follow the turns being announced. Twenty minutes later she was further out of town than she'd ever been, pulling onto a lone dirt road off the 9N. "Your destination is straight ahead," her phone announced.

Trin eased her car up the heavily tree-lined lane, gasping when she rounded the final corner. The Hardy's home was not elaborate, but a stunning plank-frame structure with a square lower level and jutting peaks, reminiscent of the old world.

Reminiscent of her old home.

IPSWICH, MASSACHUSETTS
1689

"Karina, please retrieve the potatoes from the cellar."

"Yes, Mama." Karina looked at her mother's frail frame, happy she was still alive. The spell she'd survived had changed her physically; she no longer had long raven hair, but instead, a sickly gray she always tied up in a bun. Emotionally, however, she was still the strong, loving woman the girls had always known. After their father's untimely death, their mother had been their only provider and had never left them wanting.

Returning with the few remaining potatoes, Karina gently took the knife from her mother's hand and led her to the chair by the fire. "Rest, Mama. Kara, fetch Mama her tea."

Karina finished preparing their meal, while Kara and Kenna doted over their mother, bringing her the healing tea Karina kept in full supply and covering her with a blanket.

As Karina placed the new batch of pottage on the table, their mother called them over. "Girls, gather 'round." Sitting cross-legged on the thread-bare rug, the sisters looked up into their mother's loving eyes. "I fear I do not have much time with you left." She held up a hand to stop any arguments. "My magic is almost gone and my body is becoming too fragile to contain my soul. You need to prepare to let me go."

Kenna, not so little any more, began to cry. Kara's bottom lip wavered, but she remained strong. Karina's unshed tears were accompanied by a sad smile, for she knew her mother was looking forward to her release.

"I've left the house to you, Karina. Take care of it and your sisters when I'm gone."

"Of course, Mama. Now come, let's have some food." Karina gathered her sisters around the table, while returning to her mother to feed her from the spoon.

"Karina, you are the healer and the strength of this house, and it will always recognize the duty I've placed upon you. Return to the cellar and tell me what you see."

Karina set the bowl aside and did as she was asked. The shock and joy upon her face when she returned was answered only with her mother's knowing nod. Three more potatoes had replaced the ones she'd cooked earlier this eve.

"No more than you need, but never shall you want." Her mother kissed her cheek and tasted her sweet tears.

That winter, just before Yule, they laid their mother to rest.

"Hey in there!" Jason tapped on the car window. "You okay?"

Trin shook her head and wiped at her eyes. "Yes. Sorry. I was just..." *Lost*, she thought. Lost in memories, lost in emotion, lost in her belief that she and her sisters would ever reunite.

Jason opened the door and held out his hand. "Need me to carry anything?" He nodded to the grocery bags in the passenger seat with a wink.

Trin laughed. "I couldn't show up with only wine."

"We like to eat around here, so anything you brought will

be most welcome." Jason took the bags from Trin and led her inside.

The Hardy's home was light and airy. A cozy fire roared in the old stone hearth and the most heavenly scents permeated the air.

"Trin! I'm so glad you made it," Caris exclaimed, crossing the kitchen to give her a friendly hug.

"Thanks for the invite. Like I told Jason, I didn't want to intrude on your guys' day off, but I can't deny that I'm happy to be here."

"Well, we're happy to have you. I'm just putting in the roast, did you want to join me in the kitchen?"

"Yes. If you don't mind, could I borrow a baking pan and a rack in the oven?" Trin asked, pulling the bags from Jason's hands.

"Of course." Caris washed her hands then pulled out a Pyrex dish from the cabinet, setting it on the butcher's block in front of Trin. "Need anything else?"

"Nope. That's it, I have the rest all here." Trin emptied the potatoes into the sink and pulled the peeler and knife she'd brought with her from her bag. Peeling, washing, and chopping the sweet and yellow potatoes into cubes, she layered them in the glass pan, drizzled them with olive oil, and coated them with sea salt, pepper, and a sprig of rosemary she'd brought from home.

"Those look great," Jason remarked from over her shoulder.

"They're so simple to make and taste fantastic. I hope you'll both agree."

"I have no doubt. You seem to know your way around a kitchen." Jason smiled.

The blush on Trin's cheeks reddened when she caught the grin on Caris's face.

"My stuff should be ready in an hour, how about your potatoes, Trin? How long do they need?"

"About thirty minutes at 400 degrees."

"Perfect. I'll set the timer to add them in just a bit," Caris offered.

"Would you both like a glass of wine while we wait?" Trin held up the bottle she'd brought and smiled.

"Yes, please," Caris replied as Jason retrieved three glasses from the rack.

"I hope you like moscato," Trin stated, suddenly unsure whether bringing two bottles of the same thing was the smartest choice.

"Oh, yum! I've had that kind before and loved it. Great pick, Trin." Caris's smile put her at ease.

They popped the cork and moved into the living room, chatting easily while they waited for the food to cook.

"You have a lovely home."

"Thank you," Jason replied, taking a seat next to Trin on the couch. "It's been in the family for years."

Trin looked at the river-rock chimney, up the clapboard walls to the exposed beams and sighed. It was so odd to sit in a modern home and long for one that had been gone for over three centuries. "Wait. I thought you two just moved into town?" she questioned.

"We did, but the house belongs to my father. He kept it rented until we announced we'd both be relocating to BlackBrook," Jason explained.

"Well, you're very lucky. I'd love nothing more than to live in something rooted in such history."

Caris tilted her head at Trin's comment. "Have you not always lived here, Trin?"

"Oh, I have," *In this life at least,* she thought, "except when I was attending school in the city." Trin took a sip of wine. "Where did you two live before moving to BlackBrook?"

"Massachusetts," Jason declared.

Trin's glass froze against her lips and her head started to spin. She tried to heed Kit's words, *"friends...that's all they can be,"* but something about this seemed like so much...*more.* And it wasn't just that she and Caris had similar features with their auburn hair and green eyes, but the familiarity she felt with Jason, the house, and their connection to Massachusetts. All of it seemed too important to ignore.

Trin thought back to her vision to pinpoint its origin, realizing it only happened once she'd made contact with Caris's back during her massage. She quickly ran though the events of today, and so far, they had not yet touched skin to skin; Caris's hug had been at arm's length, her forearms only touching Trin's sweater due to her kitchen-soiled hands.

Trin set her glass on the rustic coffee table and reached across for Caris's hand.

Another shock arced between them.

"Wow. I can't wait until winter is over," Caris laughed, rubbing her fingers on her jeans.

"Sorry. I was only wanting to ask if you'd like another glass of wine while I check the timer," Trin diverted.

"For sure. Thanks," Caris replied.

Trin walked into the kitchen, leaving Caris and Jason alone in the living room. She reached the island and gripped the corner. It was happening again. Visions of her and her sisters full of joy and magic filled her head.

Chapter Five

Caris grabbed Trin's elbow, again touching only the material of her sweater. "Trin, are you okay?"

"Yes, I'm sorry. I just got a little light headed for a moment."

"No more wine for you," Jason teased.

"Very funny," Trin retorted. "Really, I'm fine. I think I just got up too fast. Now let me get these potatoes into the oven, then you can give me a tour of the rest of your home, if that's okay?"

"I'd love to," Caris responded.

Trin tossed in the potatoes while Caris checked on her roast—about thirty-five minutes to go she calculated.

Caris led Trin to the backdoor and pointed. "It's hard to see buried under the snow, but we have a garden in the yard and a small shed in the back there."

Trin smiled, spotting the cute structure in the far corner that butted up to the surrounding forest. "It's truly lovely, I can't wait to see it in spring with everything in bloom." Trin shook her head. "I'm sorry. How presumptuous of me. That's if I'm invited back, of course."

Caris laughed while Jason smiled and shook his head. "Of course you're invited back, Trin." Jason ran his hand down the arm of her sweater, their fingers touching briefly, igniting yet another shock. Trin didn't pull away this time, but instead, looked deep into his eyes.

Time spun and suddenly it wasn't Jason in front of her, but her long lost love, Jeremiah Hollsteen.

IPSWICH, MASSACHUSETTS
1690

"Karina, please. Do not deny me any longer. Your sisters are old enough to get along without you, or, if need be, I will move into your home and provide a father figure to them both after we've married. I love you, Karina," Jeremiah professed.

"My sweet, Jeremiah. I love you, too, for I always have and I always will. But I fear that a terrible time is upon us. I have to remain vigilant and not get caught up in the trappings of love. I'm sorry."

Jeremiah dropped his sad eyes and hung his dark head. Karina touched his cheek, lifting his eyes to hers, then placed a sweet kiss upon his lips. "Do not despair, my love. While I cannot commit to becoming your wife, I will never deny you my heart."

Jeremiah, strong and handsome, gathered Karina in his arms and in an instant transported them to their special place, a hidden meadow deep within the Berkshires.

"I want you, Karina. Mind, body, and soul."

Their passion ignited, as did their magic, lighting up the night sky. Witches both, they weren't bound by mortal rules, freedom to love and celebrate ones wild nature had always been the pagan way. Rejoicing in the circle of life, the turning of the wheel was celebrated across the land on this Beltane night.

Earlier this same eve, hidden deep within the woods, they'd circled the maypole, secretly dancing to the drums and partaking in the cakes and ale of the ritual. Smiling coyly at one another, they kept their distance until their passion could no longer be denied. Now, here under the stars, they made wild love and cast their thanks and wishes up into the night sky.

"Trin, my god, are you okay?" Jason asked.

Trin looked up from her new location on the floor. "What happened?"

"One minute you were looking at me, and the next, you fainted."

"Here, drink this." Caris offered her a cup of tea, smelling strongly of oatstraw and rose hips. Yet another thing to alight Trin's curiosity. How did Caris know to brew her such a grounding potion?

"Thank you, I'm so embarrassed."

"No need to be embarrassed, Jason's made many a girls faint with his ridiculous adorations," Caris joked.

"Ha ha. There is nothing ridiculous about this." He looked at Trin. "You scared me. Are you sure you're okay?"

Caris moved away, leaving the two of them on the floor in front of the fire. Trin blinked rapidly as words caught in her throat. Jason smoothed the hair from her face and smiled kindly, gesturing to the cup in her hand. "Drink up."

A few more sips and Trin was once again grounded and centered. "Thank you."

Jason helped her to her feet and trailed close behind as

Trin made her way back into the kitchen. "Thanks for the tea, Caris. It did the trick." Trin smiled at the petite red-head, hoping Caris would reveal her secrets.

"No problem. I get it at a little herbal shop back home."

Back home? "Where in Massachusetts are you from exactly?"

"Ipswich." Caris winked as the oven timer went off. "Oh good, I think some food will help settle your head."

Trin couldn't agree more. This push and pull between the present and the past was becoming too much to bear. As Kit had mentioned, she'd had visions before, in other lifetimes, but not like this. Not actual memories of her former life, but more like echoes of who she used to be. This was different, and despite what Kit said, she needed to figure out why.

"Caris, do you mind if I ask you a personal question?" Trin asked as Jason returned to the living room to clear their drinks.

"Sure. Shoot." Caris smiled as she grabbed her pot holders and opened the oven door.

"With your tattoos and carefree spirit, and now seeing your home and knowing where you come from, not to mention your familiarity with herbs," Trin took a deep breath, "I'm wondering if you're Wiccan."

There. She'd blurted it out, hoping it would be the best way to go. She didn't think her tone sounded accusatory, but was left to stand nervously while Caris set the roast on the counter then returned silently to the oven to retrieve the potatoes.

"I'm sorry. Please don't be offended. I only ask because *I'm* Wiccan and thought I recognized a kindred spirit within you," Trin explained.

Caris set the pot holders down and smiled up at Trin, taking her measure. "You have good instincts. Actually, we're both Wiccan." She gestured to Jason as he returned to the room.

"You giving away our secrets, cousin?"

Caris and Jason laughed while Trin stood relieved, happy, confused, and conflicted all at once. Kit was right, it was Caris's magical energy that had drawn her and nothing more. She couldn't be Kara if Jason was her cousin, it simply didn't work that way. Trin tried to relax, popping a potato into her mouth in an effort to unclog her mind. In one way she was disappointed, hoping that somehow, she'd finally found her long lost sister. But in another, this meant that she could pursue a relationship with Jason, if that's what she wanted.

"Trin asked and I answered. Besides, like you said, I feel like I've known her forever, too. She puts me at ease, so yes, I told her our secret." Caris winked at Trin and gathered three plates from the cupboard.

The rest of the evening was pure heaven. The pork roast was tender and juicy, and Trin's golden and sweet potatoes were the perfect match. Caris had also prepared a salad and roasted carrots they'd grown and harvested themselves this past season. They talked about the root of their practices—Trin keeping her *true* story concealed, of course, then spent the remainder of the night watching movies.

At a little after eleven, Jason helped Trin to her car, depositing her bag of utensils she'd brought from home into the passenger seat.

"Thank you, again, for another pleasant evening," Trin genuinely expressed.

"You're welcome. I'm glad you came."

"Me too."

Jason leaned in, causing her stomach to flutter. The internal debate taking place in her head would have provided a decent laugh for anyone privy to her thoughts. *Cheek? Lips? Do I turn away? Say something first? Wait, no. After? Shit, what should I say?*

The brief kiss was over by the time Trin got out of her own head.

"What are you doing tomorrow?" Jason asked, taking away all the pressure.

"Nothing."

"Great. Would you like to accompany me on an adventure?"

Trin giggled. "Sure. Sounds fun."

"I'll pick you up around noon if that's okay."

"Should be fine. I'll see you then." Trin smiled and let Jason place another light peck on her cheek before backing out the drive.

The road home was fraught with rainbows and flying unicorns as her heart began to soar.

Chapter Six

He dragged the witch by the hair, deep into his cave. Disappointed in the failure of his last spell, he'd taken steps to boost his power. Feeding on the blood and magic of witches had always been his kind's only hope of survival, and he wasn't about to lose his favorite meal. She whimpered as she lay frozen on the stone floor, his knife nicking her precious flesh. "Boost my power, boost my sight, forbid the three to reunite. Blinded by blood, shielded by lies, my strength alone will forbid the rise."

Trin crept in the front door and across the living room to the kitchen, trying not to step on the squeaky plank in the floor.

"You're home late." The kitchen light flipped on.

Trin jumped. "Shit, Kit. Will you please stop scaring me?"

"Sorry. I didn't mean to scare you. I was just worried about you since the roads are getting icy again."

"Are they? I didn't notice." Trin walked to the sink and laid her bag on the counter. She'd deal with putting everything away in the morning. Right now, all she wanted to do was sleep and see where her dreams took her.

"Why are you smiling?" Kit prompted. "Oh my god, tell me everything. Did you let Officer Hardy frisk you?"

Trin burst out laughing. "Shut up! No, of course not. I had a pleasant evening with him and Caris, that's all. Now I'm going to bed. Goodnight, sister."

"Goodnight, yourself. But tomorrow, you better plan on waking up early and giving me all the details." Kit wagged a finger at her as she ascended the back stairs that led from the kitchen to their rooms.

That night, Trin dreamt of Jason and crystals, Jeremiah and ropes, Kara and water, and Caris and herbs. She tossed and turned, slipping through space and time. Sister, lover, cousin, friend. Her head spun as she tried to use her magic to break through this hellish mix of hopes and dreams, fears and regret.

But it was a final image of being devoured by a shrouded being that jolted her from the nightmare.

"Trin, wake up!"

Light poured in from the windows as Kit shook Trin's shoulders. "What's going on? What time is it?"

"Oh my god. Are you all right? I couldn't wake you." The fear in Kit's voice brought her quickly to attention.

Trin looked around the room, trying to get her bearings. *What the hell was that?* she thought. "I'm okay. Everything's okay. Calm down."

"I heard you screaming but when I tried to wake you I couldn't," Kit sobbed.

"That's so weird. I feel like I just laid down and yet obviously it's morning."

"Obviously, you're *not* okay. It's not morning...it's almost noon."

"Shit!" Trin bolted out of bed, startling Kit even further.

"What the hell are you doing?"

"I have a date."

"What? After what you just went through?"

"Relax, Kit. I didn't go through anything. I had a bad dream is all."

"Really? A bad dream that kept you locked inside your mind for hours? You're just going to blow that off for a date?" Kit's fear had turned to anger.

"There's nothing to be done now that I can't do later. When I return we'll do the scrying spell for Kara, and I'll take some time to look into my dream then. Okay?"

"Yeah, sure. Whatever."

Kit stomped from the room while Trin raced to get dressed. Thank god it was winter and she could throw on multiple layers of clothes and a hat without appearing rushed or lazy. She brushed her teeth and grabbed her camera, racing downstairs just as the doorbell rang.

"Good morning!" Trin exclaimed, out of breath.

"Good afternoon?" Jason smiled, looking down at her bare feet.

"Oh, yes. Come on in while I grab some boots."

Jason stepped over the threshold and closed the door while Trin hopped from foot to foot, pulling on her flannel-lined hiking boots. "All set."

Jason laughed. "Are you okay? You seem a bit flustered."

"No, no. I'm fine. Getting a late start is all. I'm all set. Let's go." Trin rushed Jason back out the door, wanting to avoid an awkward introduction between him and a grumpy Kit.

"So...what are we doing today?" Trin asked.

"You'll see."

"Well, as you can see," Trin held up her camera case, "I plan to document everything."

Jason's laugh washed away any lingering stain her

nightmare had left.

Snapping pictures out the window, Trin enjoyed the twenty-minute ride and was excited when they crept up to the edge of Taylor pond. Jason parked the truck then helped Trin out and onto the path that led them to a very cute, well-maintained ice shanty.

"Have you ever been ice fishing before?" Jason asked.

"Nope." Trin giggled.

"Then it truly is an adventure." Jason opened the door to the little shack. "It's not big, so be careful and mind your head."

Trin climbed in and took a seat on the futon that was placed against the wall, pulling the heap of blankets over her legs.

"Give me a minute and I'll get a fire started." He gestured to the tiny wood burning stove that sat in the corner. Its pipes were only about three inches in diameter and it was just the cutest thing Trin had ever seen. This tiny, functional little house had Trin smiling from cheek-to-cheek. She debated lighting the fire with her magic, but wasn't sure how advanced Jason and Caris were. Most Wiccan's could access magical energy, but only a select few actually become attune enough to hone it into a manifested power, at least not in this century.

Sparks flared as Jason lit the fire-starter already placed in the belly of the tiny stove with a long wooden match; within minutes the fire had taken the chill off, and it was downright cozy. Trin couldn't help but notice Jason's broad shoulders and strong arms as he took off his plaid coat and unlatched the small door in the floor of the hut. The round hole beneath was large enough for a person to fit through, and while still visible, it was now almost completely frozen over. Jason used a hefty hand-held ice auger to reopen the hole, scooping out the loose pieces with a large skimmer as he did.

"Okay. All done. Which pole would you prefer?" Jason asked, all smiles.

Trin laughed and grabbed the wooden fishing pole shaped like Tweety Bird, leaving the one shaped like a duck for Jason. "You've got a real *Grumpy Old Men* vibe going on here."

Jason's boisterous laugh filled the space as he tossed his head back. "Well, that little comment just made me love you even more. That movie is a classic and one of my all-time favorites." He wiggled his 'Green Hornet' lookalike in the air.

Trin sat straight faced, all joking aside. He'd just said he loved her, but was he being serious or was she once again taking him the wrong way?

Jason eased the tension when he placed a small peck on her cheek. "Let's get you baited up."

"Baited up?"

Jason nodded. "Yes, I'm going to be putting on a lure called a jig with some shiner minnows, and all you'll have to do is lift your pole up and down to attract the fish's attention."

"Sounds exciting!" Trin smiled.

Ten minutes passed, and she'd found that ice fishing was anything but exciting. Trin had done as instructed, bobbing the pole up and down but hadn't gotten a single bite. The cabin was warm and in the background drifted soft music from the old-time radio Jason kept on a shelf. The two were enjoying each other's quiet company and Trin quickly found herself lost in thought as she stared at the icy water.

Flashes of her past life with Jeremiah played through her mind. Memories at first, then faces of strangers twisting throughout time, always dark-haired and hazel-eyed, exactly like her lost love's. She looked at Jason and felt a connection, one that couldn't possibly be. Trin desperately wanted to grasp to the thread that was being laid out for them both, but knew it was only a desperate woman's wish. This couldn't possibly be what she was imagining. Magic or not, Jeremiah had been lost long ago.

Focused again on the developing vision, Trin closed her eyes, sighing at Jeremiah's smiling face. Contentment suddenly turned to panic, however, when the vision of Jeremiah began to frantically wave his hands in warning.

Trin's eyes snapped open. "Jason!" she screamed.

Without warning, Jason's body was slipping through the icy water as phantom hands dragged him under the frozen surface. Down, down he spiraled, away from Trin and straight towards his death.

Trin moved to dive in after him, stopping short, realizing a fool's plan. She couldn't save him if she too were dead. Trin closed her eyes and pulled what little magic she had from deep within her and placed her hands on either side of the hole. Words flew from her lips. "Break the grip of these cursed hands, return my love safely to land, feed my power, from three to one, as I will it, so shall it be done."

Trin slammed her palms on the ice, sending a massive energy blast throughout the pond. The tidal wave created sent the water rushing outward then back in on itself, forcing a solid spout to jut up through the hole that carried Jason up and out with it.

"Jason, oh god, please be okay." Trin scrambled to grab the blankets off the futon, casting flames from her fingertips to stoke the fire.

"What happened?" Jason asked through chattering teeth.

"I'm not sure. One minute everything was calm and the next you were slipping through the hole. Do you remember anything?"

"Not really," he mumbled. "Only that I became really tired all of a sudden. I must have nodded off and fell forward through the hole," he struggled to explain.

Trin stood silent, choosing to let him believe his own

version of the story. "I'm sorry. I should have been more entertaining company," she joked, trying to lighten the mood before she burst into tears.

"That's just it, Trin. I'm so comfortable around you that I find myself at peace whenever we're together. I can't explain it. I've been out here by myself with no one to talk to, yet I've never fallen asleep. You calm me, Trin." Jason professed through blue lips.

Without another word, Jason leaned in, placing his forehead against hers while taking her hands in his. Another blue spark flared at their contact, and Trin looked into Jason's heated eyes and was overwhelmed.

He had opened up his third eye to her, whether he meant to or not, and in that moment their connection became a tangible thing. She looked into his heart and mind and found Jason to be a kind and loving man. Suddenly aware of his unabashed feelings, she felt his lips on hers and didn't resist. Tentative tastes and sweet pecks quickly turned to playful nips and sensual swipes of his tongue.

Jason pulled her close, his body still cold and shivering. "They say to warm a hypothermic body you should lay skin-to-skin." Jason smiled.

"I've heard that too."

Jason raised his hands above his head, mischief playing in his eyes, as Trin lifted off his wet shirt.

Chapter Seven

Wrapped in the blankets and each other, Trin and Jason continued to kiss and cuddle, like a couple of teenagers. They'd only disrobed down to their undergarments and she refused to take it any further than that. She wouldn't allow herself to get caught up in the emotions of such an intense situation, especially one that was magically induced.

"I think you're warm enough," Trin suggested, "and we better get back soon. You need some warm soup and continued monitoring."

"Are you applying for the job?" he asked.

Trin laughed. "No, I have to get home. And I'm sure Caris will take very good care of you."

"You're right. But thanks for saving me and for the most

enjoyable body heat," Jason winked as he kicked off the covers to redress. "How did you get me out of there anyway?"

Trin froze, not sure what to say.

"All I remember is hands reaching for me. I guess that was you pulling me out, so thanks again." Jason thankfully cut her off with his own summation.

"You're welcome." Trin kept her mouth shut, buttoned her shirt, and pulled on her boots. There was no way she was going to botch a perfectly valid explanation with thoughts of evil curses and ghostly apparitions. Those same thoughts, though, raised the question; why would anyone want to hurt Jason? It made no sense.

Trin was more eager than ever to get home and address the odd things that had been happening—her strange connection to Caris and Jason, her nightmare, and now this. Something was off, and she and Kit needed to find out what.

"Thanks for the adventure!" Trin kissed Jason and jumped from the truck. "Maybe next time we can avoid the near-death experience."

"I agree. That definitely was not on the planned schedule." Jason smiled.

"I'll call to check on you tomorrow." Trin waved and sighed as he drove off, then turned and stomped the snow from her boots before entering the house.

"Kit, are you home?" Trin called from the foyer, hanging her things and proceeding to the kitchen.

"You made it back." Kit's sleepy voice sounded from over her shoulder.

"Hey! Yeah, safe and sound." Trin cringed internally at the thought of how close they came to the complete opposite of that. "Would you like some tea?" Trin offered, anxious for her own hot beverage to take the chill off.

"No thanks." Kit's clipped response cleared up whether she was still annoyed or not.

"Did you still want to do a scrying spell with me tonight?" Trin asked, hoping to soften Kit's mood.

"No. You go ahead. I'm not feeling all that well."

Hmm. Odd. Kit had never passed up the chance to work magic with her before. "What's wrong?"

"Just a bug, probably. I'll be fine with a good night's rest." Kit smiled and gave a little salute as she headed back upstairs in her flannel pjs.

Trin debated arguing for her to stay, but the thought of working alone suddenly appealed to her very much. She needed to connect to what was happening without Kit's negative influence, however reality based it was.

Trin grabbed her tea, opened the door to the cellar, and descended the stairs. The lights flickered on as she moved past each one, illuminating the space to reveal their hidden work area.

Cupboards and benches were lined with candles, herbs, oils, and bowls, all charged for sacred work. Trin took out her favorite scrying bowl and filled it with water and salt, and then placed it on the altar in the center of the room. Gathering the rest of her supplies, she lit two candles, one black for protection and banishing negativity, and one violet to connect to the Goddess for insight and clarity. Three drops of jasmine oil and a pinch of mugwort and she was ready to begin.

"Clear of mind, clear of sight, as I travel with the Goddess this night. Visions of clarity, visions of truth, uncover what's hidden, at its root."

Ripples flowed through the water as Trin focused her third eye directly on the center point. Drops of blood tendrilled across the surface, tinting the water red. The floor fell away and Trin was suddenly flying through the night sky in her astral form. Fires raged, witches hung, and ancient texts flashed through Trin's mind. Transported across time and space, she saw herself, Kara, and Kenna together, then watched as they shifted from one life to another, their faces different but their souls the same. Bound by the same energy each and every time, drawn by the heart but forced to remain apart. Outstretched hands, male and female, reached for Trin, shouting silent cries through a horde of bloody corpses.

Trin's head snapped up. Though freed from her vision, the words *'forced to remain apart'* echoed through her mind. Clarity dawned and she sucked in a breath. She hadn't been imagining things, something *was* here, and it was purposely trying to keep her from finding Kara.

Trin gave thanks to the God and Goddess and cleansed the area, replacing her tools in their proper place then raced upstairs. She debated waking Kit so they could start on a spell to reveal and block whatever was doing this, but after a quick glance at the clock, decided to wait until morning.

Tucked in, Trin gave a silent prayer. "Lord and Lady grant me peace this night, protect all I love from harm and fright. Let me wake to a brand new day, filled with joy in every way."

"Jason, what happened?" Caris demanded as she rifled through the closet for his favorite blanket.

"I'm not sure. One minute I was staring at the jig and the next, I was falling through the damn hole. Something had ahold of me, Car. A ghost or demon maybe, but it was definitely pulling me down until Trin cast her spell."

"Does she know?"

"No. I didn't want to push her and she didn't feel obliged to share."

"We're going to have to put more protection in place until we're ready," Caris warned.

"I agree. We can't keep this up much longer."

Chapter Eight

Trin woke from a peaceful sleep, ready to face the day and excited to start the spell that would break this wretched curse, if that's what it was.

"Time to rise and shine," she prompted Kit.

"Ugh...leave me be, woman," Kit groaned in response from under the covers.

"I need your help with a spell."

"Since when?"

"Since something evil is trying to keep us from finding Kara."

Kit flipped the duvet away from her face with a quick snap. "What?"

"Yeah. I did some scrying last night, and I know for a fact that something or someone is here and blocking us from finding our sister."

"You're sure?"

"Yes. I mean, I didn't see a face or name, but the odd blood rituals and dead bodies I saw in my vision were a pretty clear indication."

Kit sighed. "Katrine..."

Trin hated when she used her full name. "Don't 'Katrine' me!" Trin exclaimed. "I know what you're going to say. I'm letting my imagination run wild because I'm so desperate to find our sister, but I'm telling you...there's something going on and we need to find out what it is."

Kit tossed the rest of the blankets off and stood to face Trin. "I promise you we will get to the bottom of this, but it's going to have to wait. I'm due back at the gallery tonight and won't return until Friday morning."

"What? Why? I thought the show was only supposed to be two days?"

"It was, originally, but when Harold had to cancel and reschedule due to the weather, the gallery offered to extend the showing due to the inconvenience."

Trin felt like the petulant one now. She should be excited and proud of Kit, and she was, but the urgency of finding out what magical barrier was being cast upon their entire destiny seemed like a trump card in her book. "Fine. I'll keep searching for answers while you're gone but won't do any real magic until you return."

"Good. And don't be mad at me. I love you, Trin, and I don't want to see you hurt."

"I know. I love you, too." She hugged her sister and returned to her room, resolved to get some rest while she could.

Unable to fall asleep, Trin tossed and turned for the hour it took Kit to leave the house. When Trin heard the front door close, she pushed out of bed and slipped on her fuzzy slippers and started for the kitchen, but then stopped halfway down the stairs. Walking back into her room, she grabbed her cell phone from the night stand and looked at the display. She needed to check on Jason and hoped 9:00am wasn't too early to call.

"Hello?" Caris answered.

"Caris. Hi. It's Trin. I'm sorry to call so early, but wanted to check on Jason."

"Hi, Trin. It's fine, we're up and he's doing good. How are you holding up?"

Trin scrunched her brow at the odd question.

"I'm fine. Just a little worn out."

"Would you be up for some company? Jason insists on seeing you, but I refuse to let him out of my sight."

Trin looked around the kitchen and glanced into the living

room, making sure it was clean enough for guests. "Sure, that would be great."

"Okay, cool. Say in about an hour?"

"Perfect. I'll put something on for brunch."

Caris laughed. "Well, you know we won't say no to food."

"See you in a bit." Trin ended the call and turned to the stove. If she was going to be hosting brunch, she'd need to fix something more fitting than the bacon and scrambled eggs she'd been planning to make.

After a quick shower, Trin dressed in jeans and a sweatshirt, throwing her slippers back on for comfort. She was a wiz in the kitchen and it didn't take long for the biscuits, sausage gravy, and broiled potatoes to fill the air with a hearty aroma. She placed fruit and juice on the table just as a knock sounded from the door.

"Hi..." Trin's voice trailed off. It wasn't Jason and Caris, but a strange man Trin had never seen before.

"Forgive the intrusion, but my car has broken down and it's freezing cold."

Trin looked up and down the street, looking for the man's car but found nothing in sight. "I'm so sorry for your inconvenience. Please come in, and you can borrow the phone."

Trin paused. *Why doesn't he have a cell phone of his own? And why did he end up on my doorstep when his car's obviously not even close?*

"Actually, if you could wait here a moment, I'll fetch the phone and a cup of coffee for you." Trin held fast to the door jam, blocking his way inside.

The stranger frowned and pulled his coat tight. "Sure. I'll wait right here."

Trin closed the door and returned to the kitchen, grabbing a cup and filling it with coffee as fast as she could. Yanking the cordless phone from its cradle she returned to the door, opening it only to find Caris reaching for the doorbell.

"Hi!" Caris jumped.

Trin frowned and looked past her and Jason, in search of the man. He was nowhere in sight.

"Trin, is everything all right?" Jason asked.

"Yes, I'm sorry, please come in." Trin returned the phone to its base and set down the cup of coffee then took their coats and welcomed them to her home. "The food is almost ready. If you'd like to join me in the kitchen, I'll grab you something to drink," Trin offered.

Trin walked towards the kitchen, passing up the cup she'd set on the table by the door.

"Don't you want your coffee?" Jason asked.

Trin shook her head then gave a faint smile. "Thanks."

"Trin, are you sure you're okay? Something seems up." Jason's tone was kind but serious.

Trin sighed. "Just before you arrived, there was a man at

my door claiming to need help because his car broke down. I didn't see a car anywhere and he seemed frustrated when I asked him to wait on the stoop. When I came back with the phone and a cup of coffee, he was gone and you two were standing there instead."

"Wow. That is weird. We didn't see anyone when we drove up," Caris looked at Jason then shrugged.

"Maybe he got picked up by one of the guys. You want me to call the station and see if anyone has him?"

Trin blew out a relaxing breath. "No. That's okay. You're probably right. There's always officers cruising this street," Trin smiled, "lucky for me."

Jason laughed and Caris shared a smile with them both.

"The food smells great, you need any help?" Caris offered.

"Nope. Stay put, I'll grab everything. Help yourself to the juice and fruit." Trin set the casserole dishes on the table and sat down to join her guests.

"How are you feeling, Jason?" Trin turned to Caris. "Did his body temperature stay up throughout the night?"

"He was still a little chilled, but yes, whatever you did to warm him initially saved him, I have no doubt."

Jason smiled at Trin from across the table, bringing a blush to her cheeks. "Well, I'm glad he's okay, but I'm surprised you're both not still tucked in bed. I bet it was a long night."

"I tried to insist he stay put, but he wanted to see you and after hearing what he had to say, I thought it was best if we both came."

Trin raised her eyebrows. "Okay...what is it you have to say?"

Caris looked at Jason and nodded.

"I think that whatever happened at the pond was more than just me getting sleepy and falling in," Jason stated.

Trin blanched.

"After thinking about it more, I could actually feel hands pulling me down, so I wanted to see if you saw anything before you grabbed me."

Trin grabbed her glass of juice and took a slow drink. Jason hadn't brought up her magic, so she wasn't sure if she should either, but then again, they were all practicing witches. The problem always came when she revealed that her magic was so much more.

IPSWICH, MASSACHUSETTS
1691

"Karina, you mustn't ever tell what we are. You know our ways and the root of our belief is to *know* but to remain silent,"

Jeremiah pleaded. "There are dangerous things happening about, and I will not risk losing you, or your sisters."

"I am not a child, Jeremiah, and do not plan to go about screaming 'I'm a witch' from the hilltops, but I will not be scared into hiding my gifts when someone is in need of my help."

"It could be a trick, Karina. You've only met this woman and suddenly she needs your magical assistance with her newborn baby?" Jeremiah dropped his head, feeling the pull of what he was saying deep within his chest. He was a witch, akin to Karina, and denying someone assistance went against his nature as well. "Things are changing, my love, and we have to be more careful for it."

Karina touched his cheek and smiled, "I'll be careful, my dear. You have my word."

With one last glance at her beloved, she followed the trail to town, her basket filled with homemade remedies and magically enhanced tinctures. She ventured straight to Sarah Bishop's, as she always did, for it was her new neighbor, Ann Putnam, who was in need of assistance. Sarah had told the young girl of Karina's gifts and suggested that perhaps she try one of her potions to help cure her baby's fits. Upon arriving, Karina asked Ann to remove the baby's clothing and lay him flat on his back.

Warming her hands with oil, Karina closed her eyes and

slowly began massaging the infant's belly in a deosil motion. The women remained silent and still as Karina pulled a small vial from her skirt pocket. She unscrewed the dropper and pinched three dots of liquid onto the baby's tongue.

"This contains chamomile, fennel, caraway, and blackthorn. Place three drops on his tongue after every meal." Karina replaced the lid and handed the bottle to Ann, just as the baby ceased to cry.

Ann reached out a trembling hand and took the vial without saying a word.

"See, didn't I tell you, Ann. Our Karina here is a wonderful healer. The salves she gives me are pure magic. Magic I tell you," Sarah beamed.

Karina smiled and handed Mrs. Bishop the 'magic salves' she was gushing about in exchange for her payment, then gathered her things, ready to make her departure.

The rain had settled in, forcing Karina to pull the hood of her woolen cloak around her auburn hair as she stepped back onto the path. Turning to again bid farewell to Sarah and Ann, Karina felt a chill as she looked into Mrs. Putnam's face. The evil Karina glimpsed behind her smiling eyes sent her racing for home.

"Jeremiah! Jeremiah! You were right, and I think I've ruined us all."

Chapter Nine

"Trin. If you don't want to talk about it, it's okay," Jason offered.

"No, no. It's all right. I'm just trying to recall as many details as possible. It all happened so fast." Trin recovered. "I was relaxed and daydreaming too, and suddenly, I heard a noise and opened my eyes and saw you slipping in. I fell to my knees next to the hole and slammed my hands on either side of the ice, screaming your name. Then, once I saw your hair below me, I reached in and grabbed you by the shirt and pulled as hard as I could," Trin shrugged. "That's really all I remember."

Jason looked from Trin to Caris and took a deep breath. "Okay, well, I guess that means I'm going crazy." He shrugged.

"Thanks for having us over, now let's enjoy this fine spread, shall we?" he suggested with a half-smile.

Trin dished potatoes, biscuits, and gravy onto their plates, then tried to fill the space with generic conversation as they all enjoyed their food.

"When do you two have another day off?" Trin asked.

"Jason works the entire week, but I still have tomorrow off," Caris replied. "It's scheduled as teacher work day, but I took care of everything I had to do on Saturday, so I could have some extra time to myself."

"Good plan. What are you gonna do with the extra time?" Trin asked, trying to remain engaged.

"Actually, I was thinking of making a run to Ipswich to get some supplies. Would you like to come with?"

Trin's smile lit up the room. "Caris, that sounds fantastic. Let me make sure I can move any appointments I have for tomorrow, but yes, I would love to join you."

"Well, that sounds like a party. Wish I could come," Jason added.

"I wish you could too," Trin replied shyly.

"How about this? I'll let my cousin steal you away tomorrow, but come Friday night, you're all mine." Jason winked.

Caris laughed and began clearing the plates as Jason reached for Trin's hand. Blue sparks erupted as their fingers met, knocking them apart.

"What the hell?" Caris gasped.

"Wow. That one was a doozy." Jason shook out his fingers.

"You mean it's happened before?" Caris asked.

Jason looked at Trin and she nodded. "Yes. Practically every time we touch," he stated flatly.

"I wasn't sure you noticed," Trin replied.

"Oh trust me, I noticed. I told you, Trin. It's like I've known you all my life, and when we touch, not only is there an actual spark, but there's also a spark I feel inside. I can't explain it."

Trin stared at the two cousins and felt her heart sink. This couldn't be anything more than magical energies recognizing and reacting to each other. Kit had warned her that she would get hurt again if she kept thinking there was more to it than that. So, resolved to spare herself any more pain, Trin accepted that this man was a fellow witch that she had a true connection with and nothing more. And right now, that worked for her.

"I feel a spark too, Jason." Trin reached for his hand again. "Actually, with both of you. I feel like our energies recognize each other, and I couldn't be happier to have found two more witches whose company I enjoy."

"Two *more* witches?" Caris prompted.

"Yes. My roommate and friend, Kit, is also a witch. You'll

get to meet her this weekend." Trin nodded to Jason.

"That's awesome. Honestly, I thought Jason and I were going to be the only Wiccans in town. So cheers to that!" Caris raised her glass of orange juice and smiled.

"Perhaps we should add a bit of champagne and make this toast official," Jason teased.

"Oh no you don't. No alcohol for the recovering patient," Caris's tone was serious, despite the smile on her face.

"Would you like to see our work space?" Trin offered.

"Absolutely," Caris remarked.

"We'd be honored," Jason added.

Caris helped Trin finish clearing the food, then followed her down into the cellar. She and Jason's sacred space was located in the shed at the corner of their land, and often times she wondered if they should convert a space indoors, like Trin had, for the convenience.

Jason stood, watching the girls as Trin showed Caris her stock and stores. Gray washed stone walls, wood shelves and cabinets lined with candles and oils. Dried herbs hung from a wooden lattice overhead, and a beautifully carved wood altar sat on a hand-woven rug patterned with stars and moons in the center of the room.

"This is lovely, Trin." Caris spoke humbly. "Truly, such a perfect space."

"Thanks." Retrieving a piece of paper from the cupboard

drawer, Trin lifted a quill and began to scribble down the list of items she planned to look for on their trip to Ipswich.

Candles, yarrow, mugwort, and rose petals.

"Looking for something?" Jason asked from over Trin's shoulder.

"Yes, as a matter of fact I am." Trin was impressed with his knowledge of her intended use of the ingredients, but as with every other life, she couldn't elaborate.

"I prefer the pendulum to scrying, personally." Caris pulled her pendulum from her pants pocket. It was a delicate pink rose quartz point with a beaded gem half way up its chain.

Trin stepped closer to inspect the bead but stopped short when the crystal started to spin wildly in Caris's hand.

Trin looked up at Caris. "Did you ask it a question?"

"Yes, in my head."

"What did you ask?" Trin demanded.

"Whether you'd find what you're looking for," Caris replied with a somber face.

"I assume that's not your 'yes'," Trin replied.

"No, but it isn't my 'no' either. I'm not sure what's happening. It's never done this before."

Trin stared at the pendulum and became lost in the connection between it and Caris. "Slow and steady, find your way. Reveal the answer, and do not sway. Truth to truth, from the highest light, answer your mistress, proof of right."

Trin blinked, freeing herself from the involuntary spell that had just flowed from her lips. Caris and Jason were staring at her with gaping mouths.

Trin's aura was glowing and the pendulum was frozen solid in midair, pointing straight at Caris's chest.

"What. The. Hell?" Jason's breathless question mirrored Trin's thoughts exactly.

Chapter Ten

Ice clung to his boots as he stomped around the cave. Desire and need drove him, but it was anger that pierced his soul. He refused to let centuries of work be all for naught. He cast the stones then slid the knife across his mangled wrist once again, to add the final ingredient. "Bound by time, her soul and mine. Cast astray, day after day. I will not falter, I will not fail, charge these words by the crimson veil."

"Holy shit! I've never seen anything like that!" Caris exclaimed as the pendulum flew from her hand.

"Damn, Trin. You're something special," Jason stammered.

"Yeah, um...I don't know what that was, it just kinda came over me."

"Well, you were definitely channeling something, you lit up like a glow worm," Jason teased.

Trin smiled and hoped they didn't dig for a more solid explanation. "Well, whatever it was, I think I could use that drink now."

"I'm down for that," Caris added, casting a speculative look in Jason's direction.

Trin gathered her list and put away her quill, then led them back upstairs.

"Actually, Trin, I think we'll take a rain check. Jason needs to get some rest and I still have a few things to finish before our trip tomorrow." Caris's smile was genuine but it didn't effectively hide her nerves.

"No problem. I've got a stack of laundry to get through and need to call the Center to rearrange my appointments. Thanks for coming over, though." Trin felt awkward but relaxed when both Caris and Jason hugged her before they left.

"I'll call you later," Jason added with a wink.

Trin closed the door, then turned and raced back to the cellar. She opened the carved wooden box atop the cupboard and pulled out her favored tarot deck. Rapidly shuffling the cards, she practically threw them onto the altar. Three cards; one for past, present, and future.

Trin acknowledged the Magician card as her past, no surprises there. But the present and future cards had her undivided attention.

The Seven of Swords indicated deceit and deception surrounding her present, while the reversed Tower forewarned her of major changes where she could no longer count on those close to her.

Trin took a deep breath and focused her third eye on the second image, hoping it would reveal its secrets.

Flashes of bone and hair slashed through her mind like pictures reflected on sharp shards of glass. Blood and stone, and now three ghostly apparitions. Astral images of her and her sisters all fighting something and always losing.

Trin sucked in a breath and broke the connection, worried she'd make contact with this evil before she was ready. She promised Kit not to do real magic until her return, and after what she'd just witnessed, Trin would definitely be waiting for her sister before casting circle to look any further.

"What was that?" Caris's voice sounded behind her.

Trin jumped. "Oh my god, Caris, you scared me."

Caris was standing stock still and white faced. "What was that, Trin?" she repeated.

"What do you mean? I was just doing a quick reading for myself. And no offense, but why are you here? I thought you and Jason were headed home."

"We were until I remembered my pendulum was lying in your cellar. I knocked and you didn't answer, so I came in and announced I was coming down. Didn't you hear me?"

"No. I was lost in my vision, I guess." Trin reached under the altar and retrieved Caris's pendulum from where it had previously fallen. "Here you go."

"Thanks. And I don't mean to pry, but you say you were having a vision, but how can that be if I saw it too?"

Trin gasped. "What do you mean?"

"I saw three faint images locked in a never-ending battle, playing out in the middle of the room, like a movie projected against a wall of fog."

"You saw it? Here in this room?" Trin shivered.

"Yes. Exactly what kind of witch are you, Trin?"

Trin stood, dumfounded, debating if she should share her secret with Caris or not. Kit's words from another lifetime, however, rang loudly in her ears. *"You revealed yourself once and ended up on a pyre. Keep silent, sister."*

"I don't know what you mean, Caris. I'm a Wiccan witch, same as you."

Caris grabbed Trin's shoulders. "No. I don't think so, Trin. You're special and I'm so glad to have you as a friend."

80

Trin fell into Caris's embrace, then waved goodbye as she retreated up the stairs. Had she dodged another bullet? Only time would tell.

IPSWICH, MASSACHUSETTS
1693

"Karina, please calm down. What are you saying, 'you've ruined us all'?" Jeremiah asked.

"I've just returned from Sarah Bishop's where I eased an infant's colic cries for her new neighbor, Ann Putnam. I couldn't help myself, Jeremiah, the baby was in so much pain."

"You're a healer, Karina, how could you possibly do anything but?" He placed a kiss atop her head.

"When I gave the mother a tonic to use, she accepted it finely, but as I took my leave I saw an evil about her, hidden behind her eyes."

Kara and Kenna walked into the kitchen as Jeremiah began to respond. Karina shook her head to silence him, not wanting to worry the girls.

"Have you heard?" Kara asked conspiratorially.

"Heard what?" Karina replied.

"A baby has died in the village and the mother is demanding the head of a witch."

Karina swooned and fell into Jeremiah's arms.

"Who's baby?" Jeremiah demanded.

"Margret Danforth's."

Karina took a deep breath and looked into Jeremiah's eyes, knowing no good would come from the deed she'd just done.

Chapter Eleven

"I have no doubt, Jason. It's her," Caris confirmed.

"I thought so too, Caris, at first. But if it is, then why hasn't she recognized us? I always thought once we found one another the veil would fall and our souls would sing in recognition."

"You know why! We've been fighting for this for centuries. Always searching, always being thwarted. But this time...we're close. How else do you explain the increased attacks?"

"I don't know, Caris. But just because Trin is powerful, it doesn't mean she's the one. A spark here and there doesn't compare to soul singing," Jason stated flatly.

"I suppose you're right, but there's something definitely going on with her. She has power unlike any other I've seen. Her vision was made real, playing out right before my eyes. She shrugged it off when I asked about it, but I'm telling you, she's special."

"I agree she's special, Caris, but I'm not convinced she's the one we've been looking for."

Caris dropped onto the couch, "I'm tired, Jason. It's been centuries since I lost my magic. At what point do we give up?"

Jason moved to take her hand. "I'm tired too, but I'll never give up. Let's get some rest and I'll do another seeking spell once the moon rises. You take Trin to Ipswich as planned and we'll continue to live our lives as we always have. Our time will come."

"Thanks again for inviting me, Caris. I'm so excited for this trip." Trin beamed.

"Of course. I usually try to get back home at least a couple times a year to restock. I mean, I know there are closer stores where I could find what I need, but there's something special about going home to the place where you first discovered your magic," Caris smiled.

You have no idea, Trin thought. She hadn't yet returned to Ipswich in any of her previous lifetimes, mainly because of the worry of how it would affect her. But today, she felt ready.

"Do you still have family in the area?" Trin asked.

"No, not anymore," Caris's sad smile answered any further questions Trin had. She'd lost family too, and that's probably why they relocated to BlackBrook—to escape the pain.

They spent the next five hours chatting about anything and everything as the chilled landscape of Vermont and New Hampshire passed them by.

"Getting close now," Caris announced as they turned on to MA-133.

Trin squirmed in her seat as they made their way to the heart of the small town. The landscape, though covered in snow, still held a familiar air. The brick buildings maintained an old-world feel, as did the John Whipple house that now sat at 53 S. Main Street.

Trin chuckled. This First Period house she visited as a child had been moved and was now a museum. It had obviously been expanded sometime after her hasty and necessary departure in 1693, since the original structure consisted of only a half-house timber frame with a chimney on the right side. Now, the beautiful three-story wood frame home stood proudly with two gables and casement windows containing hand-blown glass. Trin's excitement was almost palpable as information continued to free-flow into her mind.

A few turns later, they reached a small brick storefront located at the very end of what would be considered the shopping district, if Ipswich had such a thing.

"Here we are." Caris turned off the car and grabbed her purse. "Thought we'd get to the good stuff first, then we can go have a late lunch at the Clam Box if you'd like."

Trin smiled and opened her door. "That sounds fantastic."

Following Caris inside, Trin felt transported the moment she crossed the threshold. Herbs hung overhead, and the roughly plastered walls were lined with shelving units, dressers, and tables. The one to her immediate left held dark brown vials of oil, each within its own small cubby. There were consecrated candles atop silver platters, along with wands and athames lying atop a beautifully carved antique dresser to her right. Statues of multiple gods and goddesses were sprinkled throughout, some Greek, some Egyptian, and even Hindu, but the energy here was no doubt pagan. A *true* witch, like herself, owned this shop.

"Trin, I'd like you to meet, Lillian. She's the owner of this lovely shop and a dear friend," Caris announced.

"It's lovely to meet you, Lillian. Your store is wonderful." Trin shook Lillian's hand, sensing her magic the moment they touched.

Lillian's eyes sparked and she replied, "It's nice to meet you too, Trin. Feel free to gather what you need, and enjoy your time in Ipswich."

"Thank you." Trin smiled at Lillian and Caris, then continued her exploration of the shop. It was much larger than it appeared from the street.

As Trin combed her way over each and every surface, she began to see a pattern. Some things mundane and commercial, such as a vial full of purple glitter claiming to be fairy dust, sat alongside others of true power like the jeweled pendant humming beneath her hand. It was a smart thing to do, for only a true witch would know the difference. Perhaps a dedicated Wiccan, such as Caris and Jason would feel a pull towards the objects of old, and even a tourist could pick something up by mistake not knowing what they had, but everything here would do no harm, regardless of who purchased it.

Trin chuckled internally as she reached the back of the store and noticed the locked cabinet draped behind a thick curtain. *This* was where Lillian kept the off-limit items. Trin pulled back the edge of the curtain and examined the contents. The bone fragments and human hair were of no concern to her, but the charred piece of a demon's tooth rang with warning. The room started to spin, then Trin felt a hand on her shoulder.

"Steady there," Lillian remarked. "You best come away from the case or you'll have that demon's tooth lodged in your neck, looking for another meal."

"Another meal?" Trin ran a hand down the side of her throat.

Lillian guided Trin to a cozy sitting area near the office. "With the level of power you possess, I'm surprised you don't know."

"Know what?" Trin demanded.

"Our history." Lillian stated flatly.

Trin rubbed a hand down her arm to dampen the nervous energy buzzing under her skin.

"Long ago, a race of demons whose only means of survival depended upon the consumption of a witch's magic, decimated our line. Hunted as nothing more than a meal for the demons, all witches fled into a deep hiding. Protection spells were set in place by the remaining elders and the use of magic was practically forbidden."

Trin sat wide-eyed and slack-jawed, listening to the story of her people.

"The elders feared any magical energy would call the demons to them, so they kept themselves hidden from the world, forced only to watch as it changed."

"Changed how?"

"Without a ready food source, the demons began to die out. Forced to find other means of survival, they began to not only feed upon a witch's power, but learned to use it to cast their own spells—locator spells, mainly, that would lead them to their next victim."

"Demons casting witches spells?" Trin shook her head, appalled.

"Yes. But once the new world began to fill with men, Christianity gained a foothold and gave the demons another option. In a last desperate attempt, a powerful demon cast a spell to shapeshift into a human man that would change our history forever."

"What man?"

"Henrich Kramer."

Trin gasped. "The author of the Malleus Maleficarum was a demon?"

"Yes. What better way to root out any remaining magic than to incite a public witch hunt?"

Chapter Twelve

"Heinrich Kramer, the *man*, was known to have died in 1505, but the demon behind the face was forced into hiding when most of the witches on trial weren't real witches at all. He and the remaining demons took the few true witches of the time and learned to siphon their magic in smaller amounts, barely surviving until one witch casted a spell so powerful, they all came running."

"Who?"

"You, *Karina*. Your spell is what pulled us all through time."

Trin jumped from the chaise, fear coursing through her veins as she caught Caris's eye from across the room.

"What's wrong, Trin? Are you okay?" Caris called.

"I think I gave her a start with the tarot reading I did," Lillian interjected, pointing to the cards that suddenly appeared on the table between them.

"Uh oh, did you just find out you're gonna marry my cousin? I'd be freaked out too if I was you," Caris joked.

Trin looked back and forth between the women, trying to gauge what had just happened. Could Lillian truly be a witch from her time? And if what she said was true, that meant it was her fault that witchcraft in the old world had died out. Her spell had scattered her line and their natural-born powers to the wind, forcing them to soul travel aimlessly throughout time, exactly like her and her lost sisters.

Trin wiped the tears from her eyes and forced a smile onto her face. "No, no. It wasn't anything like that. I just recovered a little piece of my history that hit me hard, that's all."

"Learning the darkness of one's past only helps to bring light to their future." Lillian smiled kindly.

Trin nodded and glanced again at Caris. She wouldn't be sharing this information with her—it wasn't for a novice. She had no need to know of such things as true witches and magic eating demons. "Thanks again, for bringing me here, Caris. I'm so very grateful." Trin smiled, pretending not to be shaken to her core by all that had transpired.

"You're welcome," Caris said. "Now let's get our stuff and

go get something to eat. I'm starting to get light headed."

"Let me know if there is anything you need that you don't see," Lillian offered.

"I've found more than I expected and can't thank you enough." Trin turned away and began to gather the items on her list, adding a few power objects that seemed to be calling to her in the moment. The pendant from before, a jar of high-quality healing salve, and a ceremonial blade.

The girls met at the checkout counter, placing their items in front of Lillian to be packaged.

"Here are the keys, go ahead and load up and I'll be right out," Caris said, tossing the jumble of silver towards Trin.

"Okay. Thanks again, Lillian. It was such a pleasure to meet you." Trin took her bags and walked to the door.

"You're very welcome, and I look forward to seeing you again."

Trin smiled and set off with a wave.

Caris snapped her head towards Lillian. "Did you tell her?"

"Yes. I told her everything."

"What did she say?"

"What do you mean? You saw how shocked she was. She had no idea," Lillian snapped.

"This isn't good. It's like she can sense some things but not others. I'm going to need the tooth, Lillian."

"I don't think that's a good idea, Caris."

"I don't have any other choice. I have to see if I'm right and figure out what's blocking her. Jason and I are running out of time."

Lillian walked towards the cabinet in the back, slowly pulling out a small golden key from her pocket. She unlocked the glass door and reached for a black box on the top shelf. After filling it with crushed rue, Lillian picked up the demon's tooth with a black satin cloth and placed it inside the box.

"Here. Keep it in the box until you're ready to do the spell. It will need to be done on the next new moon, NOT the full moon. Understand?" Lillian demanded as she handed Caris the box.

"Yes, I understand. Thanks for your help. We'll be through this soon."

"I hope so, child."

Caris took her shopping bag and quickly headed to the car. "Thanks for warming it up, I had to place a special order for a statue Jason's been wanting."

"No problem. You ready to eat?" Trin asked.

"Absolutely." Caris drove straight to the Clam Box, hoping she could get Trin to confide in her over their meal.

"I haven't had a good bowl of 'chowda' in years," Trin laughed as they were directed to their seats.

"Well, you won't be disappointed. I love this place."

"Ipswich is fantastic. Do you miss it?" Trin asked, silently answering her own question. *Desperately.*

"I do, but what we have in BlackBrook is wonderful as well. I'm thrilled to have found a place where the history doesn't impede the future." Caris scoffed. "If that even makes sense."

"It does. I can see how being a witch here must be hard. Lillian has done a good job at commercializing her store to make it attractive to tourists, but in reality, the need to hide still falls heavy over this land." Trin's eyes started to glaze over.

IPSWICH, MASSACHUSETTS
1693

"It's your turn, I delivered the last batch," Kenna moaned.

"Be still, Kenna, I'll do it. You don't have to whine like the dog," Kara snapped.

The girls finished placing the last of the glass jars full of herbal creams and healing salves into the waiting baskets. Mrs. Bishop was expecting her delivery tonight, and the girls never passed up an opportunity to use their gifts to help those in need, and it didn't hurt that they'd make a few shillings in the process. Kara took hold of the designated set and started out the door.

"Just a moment, let me put on the finishing touches," Karina's soft voice drifted from behind her.

Stepping into the evening breeze, Karina placed her hands above the wicker basket and muttered softly. "Blessings within, blessings without, created with love by servants devout. Bringing light to ease one's plight, that is the goal of our gift tonight."

A golden glow illuminated the jars as the wind picked up, blowing the girls' auburn hair towards the night sky. Kenna laughed, and Kara smiled at her big sister. "That was lovely, Karina."

"Thank you. Now be on your way. We don't want to keep Sarah waiting."

Kara set off, while Kenna helped Karina replace the stocks of lavender, orris root, and camellia back upon the shelves of their small workspace in the back room. Tidying and arranging the herbs and oils for next week's batch of tinctures and charms always brought a sense of peace to Karina, one that seemed to settle over the entire house.

Inhaling deeply, Karina smiled at her sister as she moved to take the boiling kettle of cinnamon, cloves, and oranges off the fire, to prepare for this evening's meal. Kenna chopped carrots, potatoes, and cabbage for the pottage, while Karina saw to the bread.

As she placed the boiling pot above the fire, a knock on the door set their hound alight, startling them both.

Kenna grabbed the mutt and hid in the backroom, while Karina wiped her hands on her apron and crossed to the door. As she reached for the handle, a loud crack of a boot blasted the wood from its hinges.

"Witch! We've seen your magic with our own eyes. You are now officially accused and claimed in the name of God for your assault on all that is natural in this world," bellowed the loud voice of Thomas Danforth. Four men rushed inside, grabbing Karina by the arms and legs, while two others looked for anyone else in the house. Karina shook her head at Kenna, who remained hidden from view as a result of her quick spell. "Hold her down," instructed Danforth.

Karina screamed and convulsed under their hands, stilling only when they ripped her dress open, exposing her back. They were looking for the 'devil's mark' no doubt, and she knew they would most likely deem her birthmark the tell-tale sign of guilt. But, regardless of where they pulled their *truth* from, they were in fact accurate in their judgment. Karina was a witch, and deep within her bones she knew the whole town would know it before this night was over.

"Trin? Are you ready to order?" Caris asked from across the table.

"I'm so sorry, yes, please." Trin took the menu and quickly placed her order for a small bowl of clam chowder and a mini meal of the Clam Box's famous fried native clams. "I think the long drive is finally catching up to me," Trin confessed as she smiled at Caris.

Caris made her selections with the waitress, handing back their menus and offered Trin an understanding smile. "I was thinking the same thing. Do you want to get a room instead of driving back tonight, or do you have appointments tomorrow you need to return for?"

"No. I cleared my schedule until Wednesday so I'm free, but what about you? Doesn't school resume tomorrow?"

"Yes, but I keep a sub-folder in my desk in case of emergencies. If I call in before four, they'll be able to assign a substitute with no problem."

Trin pondered the thought. Would it be wise to remain here after what Lillian had told her? If she was practical, she'd race home to coordinate with Kit to substantiate Lillian's story. But, Kit was still out of town and if Trin was being honest with herself, she didn't want to hear how ridiculous Kit thought Lillian's claim was or have to deal with her jealousy about the time she spent with Caris.

"Actually, I'd love to stay another night," Trin announced.

"Great! If you'll excuse me for a moment, I'll go make the call."

Trin watched Caris walk out the front door of the restaurant, then picked up her own phone.

Trin: *How's the show going?*

Kit: *Good. How are things there?*

Trin: *Fine. Really need to talk when you get back, though.*

Kit: *I'm all yours come Friday. :) <3*

Caris returned to the table as Trin returned her phone to her purse. "All set." Caris smiled.

"Do you have a specific place you prefer to stay when you're here, or do we need to hunt down the nearest Motel 8?" Trin laughed.

"I thought we'd stay at The Inn at Castle Hill."

Trin fell back against her chair, lost again in another memory. Daniel Epps had owned Castle Hill during Karina's youth and had allowed many pagan celebrations to take place upon his grand lawn in front of the lavish country estate, the last being Beltane, where she and Jeremiah danced around the maypole.

Trin blinked to find Caris staring at her with genuine curiosity written all over her face.

"That would be lovely," Trin agreed, giddy as a schoolgirl.

"Excellent. I'm glad you're excited. The Inn is one of my

favorite places on earth."

Mine too, thought Trin. *Mine too.*

Chapter Thirteen

Wood splintered against the cave wall. "Damn that witch!" He grabbed his cauldron and threw all the shards of wood and glass into it that had gathered as a result of his anger. "I will not be thwarted." Mixing the potion had required three days, but now as the liquid boiled black, he was ready to cast his most powerful spell yet. "Dark as night, blinded be, seeping into each of thee. Cut their tie, bind their will, sacrifice the one that's nil." Black smoke filled the cave, churning and twisting into something very much alive. His maniacal laughter echoed off the stone as the caustic tendrils drifted into the night sky.

Caris and Trin finished their meal then traveled the eleven minutes down High Street to Argilla Rd, climbing the beautiful hill to reach the Crane Estate. The Castle itself, now a Tudor Revival, boasted twenty-one outbuildings, one of which served as the Inn.

Trin gazed out the car window, awestruck by the opulence that surrounded her. The mansion and landscape had changed so much since her last true visit, and she couldn't wait to explore the infamous Rose and Italian Gardens with their fountains, statues, and columns, even under the winter chill.

"Oh, Caris. This is so beautiful. I wish we had more time to spend here."

"We can always come back, you know," Caris offered.

Trin looked at her friend, "You're right of course, and next time we'll bring Jason and Kit. It would be so much fun exploring together."

"Let's get checked in, then we can light a fire and order some late tea."

"That sounds perfect," Trin beamed. Being back on her native soil was doing wonders for her mood. She couldn't wait to return when it was warmer and sink her feet back into the sand upon which she played as a child. The now public beaches were private back then, but that didn't stop a few determined children. Trin chuckled internally at the thought of she, Kara, and Kenna splashing in the waves as they each made a wish upon a seashell, spelling them to glow as they skipped over the water's surface.

Check-in was quick and easy, and their room was quaint and comfortable. "I can't believe what a joy this little day trip has turned out to be." Trin turned towards Caris. "Thank you, again, for bringing me here."

"It's always heartwarming to come home," Caris winked with a gleam in her eye.

Trin's curiosity at the innuendo was on the rise when Caris's cell phone rang from within her pocket.

"Hey, cuz. What's up?" Caris asked.

"What? Oh my god, Jason, are you all right?"

Trin sat on the bed, waiting for the news as Caris paced the room.

"Where were you when it attacked?" Caris demanded, her voice rising and full of panic.

Attacked? Oh no. This did not sound good. Trin's first thought was an accident relating to his job as a police officer, but something in her gut told her that was not the case. This was magical. Trin could feel it in her bones.

Darkness speckled her vision, and the room began to spin as Trin fell backwards onto the bed. Her eyelids fluttering as images overtook her.

Jason was walking back to the house from the shed when he was suddenly surrounded by a thick, black fog. Fingers coalesced from the mist then closed around his throat. He dropped to his knees, fighting to stay coherent as the life was being choked from his body. Dropping a hand to the ground, he spotted a jagged piece of tourmaline. Digging through the snow with his bare fingers he retrieved the shard and impaled the "hand" that was crushing his windpipe.

Trin snapped to when Caris cried out. "We're coming home right now. Stay in the house and we'll be there as soon as we can."

Trin only nodded when Caris finally looked at her.

Luckily, they were able to explain the emergency to the innkeeper and didn't have to pay for the brief visit. They were out the door and on the road within minutes.

"I'm so sorry, Trin."

"Don't you dare apologize. Jason thought something was after him at the pond, and now, with this...we need to get back."

Caris drove in silence while Trin spent the next few hours lost in her own head. She was worried about Jason, of course, but suddenly she began to question why she felt invested in something that was happening with people she had only just met? She supposed it could be chalked up to the connection they felt through their magical energy, but Trin now wondered if she wouldn't be better off distancing herself from the entire situation. Demons, magical curses, and phantom attacks weren't something she needed to add to her plate.

Four hours later, resolved, Trin backpedaled and asked Caris to drop her off at her house first, making the excuse of wanting to give the two of them their privacy. Waving goodbye, she unlocked the door and exhaled a sigh of relief when she was safely within the confines of her own home.

Casting a finger at the fireplace, Trin moved to make herself a much needed drink. No tea tonight, whiskey was called for and very much appreciated once it flowed down her throat and warmed her belly. She slipped into a deep meditation, grounding and re-centering herself while she waited for Kit's return.

"Tell me everything," Caris snapped.

Jason sat on the couch, staring into the fire with a drink in his hand. "I'd just finished another seeking spell and was returning to the house when a thick, black fog crept out from the edge of the woods." Jason shivered. "I could feel something evil writhing within it. By the time I'd cast my protection outward, it had me surrounded."

"If it was fog, why couldn't you simply brush past it and run into the house?"

Jason gave Caris an exasperated look. "Don't you think I would have done that if I could? Didn't you hear me say it was laced with evil? The damn thing turned solid and grabbed me around the throat."

"Oh my god. Like, the whole thing was solid, like a person?"

"No, it was like part of the mist *became* a hand."

Caris pulled her knees to her chest and hugged herself tight. "What did you do?"

"I was gasping for breath and fell to my knees. Luckily, I saw a piece of the tourmaline we'd used in our protection spell lying on the ground, so I grabbed it and stabbed it into the hand. A strange wailing sound filled the air, then the whole damn thing just disappeared."

"Holy crap!"

Jason nodded. "You were right...I think this means we're finally close."

"God, I hope so."

Chapter Fourteen

IPSWICH, MASSACHUSETTS
1693

Karina began to kick and scream again, trying to fight her way free from the hands that gripped her. "Here! The devil's mark," Danforth spat. The small crowd of men jerked forward and loaded her onto a wagon, securing her hands and feet roughly with ropes.

Karina met Kenna's eyes from behind her cloaked position and shook her head. *Do nothing, little one. I will take care of this,* Karina whispered into her mind as the wagon jerked. Karina closed her eyes as she cast the same warning to the absent

Kara, *"Do nothing. I will be fine."*

Her insides were jostled and jumbled by the bumps in the road, so much so, that Karina found comfort in being removed from the wagon and thrown into jail where she would await her "trial." She knew there was no escaping after Deputy Governor Danforth himself had witnessed her magic. She assumed he was hiding in the bushes when she blessed the contents of Mrs. Bishop's basket, probably tipped off by the young Mrs. Putnam, whom she'd recently helped.

Karina shook her head. Assumptions weren't going to help her, nor would anger or blame. She needed to figure out what to do and when would be the most prudent time to act.

Rats scampered over Karina's feet as she tried to sleep on the cold stone floor, dragging pieces of water-soaked bread through the bars and back to their babies. She couldn't fault them for taking care of their families, and after a night of contemplation, she'd be doing the same. She wouldn't use her magic to break free or to alter the weak-minded prosecutor's thoughts, no, she couldn't risk the fall-out, knowing her sisters would be the next pair on the pyre or hung from the nearest tree. She would stand at the stake and brave their *justice*, proud and free.

The metal door creaked open and in walked Jeremiah. This she had not counted on, and it weakened her resolve.

"Why did you come?"

"How could I not? I love you, Karina. So be it if I get caught using my magic to reach you. If you're going to burn, I'll burn with you." Jeremiah enveloped her in his arms, holding her close as she sobbed into his chest. "We'll figure a way out of this, I promise," he swore.

"No, we won't. Nothing I do will keep me from the stake. I've accepted it and so should you."

"I can't let them hurt you." Jeremiah kissed her hair, pulling her tight.

"You don't have a choice. But what I do need is your promise. Swear to me that you'll always look after my sisters. Protect them when I'm gone."

"I swear it."

Karina placed a soft kiss on Jeremiah's lips and pulled herself together. "They'll be here soon, you must go."

Jeremiah kissed his beloved again, looking back one last time as the metal door clanked shut just before he disappeared.

Ripped from the memory, Trin folded the sheets and placed the hot stones back in their basin as her timer beeped. "That concludes our session, Ms. Thompson, I'll meet you outside with some water when you're ready."

Trin escorted her last client of the day out of the Wellness Center then quickly tidied her room, anxious to get home. Kit confirmed that she should be there no later than three o'clock and it was nearly two-thirty now. Trin had several practiced conversations already laid out in her head, hopeful that Kit's reaction would be one of urgency. If there was a time they needed their full magic returned, it was now.

Caris had reported that Jason was recuperating just fine, and that they were setting more protections in place. She asked if Trin would like to join them in their castings, but fortunately she had to work and was able to kindly decline. The idea of working magic with anyone but Kit wasn't sitting right with her. Maybe it was Lillian's wild tale, or the fact that all her readings indicated there were influences present that couldn't be trusted, but until Trin had a clearer understanding of what they were facing, she would follow her gut and hunker down at home.

Kit had the fire lit and two glasses of wine poured when Trin walked through the door. "Welcome home!" Kit joyously announced. "We're celebrating."

Trin laughed and picked up her glass from the table. "Celebrating what?"

"I sold three paintings this week. It was a huge commission."

"Congratulations, Kit! I'm so proud of you."

"Thanks. Now come sit and tell me what I missed."

Trin set her glass on the coffee table, removed her coat and shoes, then snuggled into her favorite oversized chair. Ten minutes later, Trin had relayed all that transpired on her visit to Ipswich.

"That's quite a story." Kit sipped her wine.

"I know, right? I couldn't do any soul searching while Caris was there, so I couldn't verify if Lillian was truly from our time or not, but have you ever heard of anything like this during our other lives?"

"No. This is definitely a first." The look on Kit's face confirmed the news upset her as much as it had Trin.

"Do you think we should take a trip to Ipswich together and see what we can find out?"

"Possibly, but not yet. Let's just continue to look for Kara, because whatever evil or demon that's being cited, won't stand a chance against the three of us once we're reunited."

"I couldn't agree more." Trin raised her glass then downed the rest of her wine.

"I'm beat from my trip, so how about we start in the morning?" Kit suggested.

"That's perfectly fine with me. I'll whip up something for dinner and then we can both hit the hay early. Clear minds and all. How about some chicken parm?"

"Sure. Sounds great." Kit followed Trin into the kitchen and set her wine glass in the sink.

"Can you grab me the baking dish from down there?" Trin pointed to where she kept all the pans.

Kit opened the cabinet door and retrieved the dish, almost dropping it when its weight proved too heavy for only one hand.

"Whoa. You got it?" Trin asked.

"Yes. Here you go," Kit awkwardly offered Trin the dish, balancing it against her stomach and pushing it onto the counter.

"What's wrong with your other hand?" Trin asked, just now noticing Kit was nursing her left.

Kit cast Trin a weary look, then pulled her hand from beneath the sleeve of her sweater. The glamour Kit placed on it had disappeared with the pain, revealing a mass of black and blue. "I smashed it the gallery. I was helping to pack up the painting and caught myself with a hammer."

"Oh my god, Kit! Why would you hide this from me?" Trin grabbed Kit's injured hand and began to chant healing words in an effort to ease her pain.

"With everything that's been going on, I didn't want to worry you."

Trin looked into Kit's eyes and saw the unshed tears starting to build.

"Well, it's not broken, but it is badly bruised and is obviously going to be super sore for a while."

Kit slowly pulled out of Trin's grasp. "Thanks. I'll be fine."

Trin's skeptical glance had Kit raising her eyebrow in response. Whether it be in this life or their previous ones, Kenna had always been stubborn, a trait Trin appreciated but hated all the same.

"Wrap it up and put some salve on it before bed," Trin instructed.

"I will. Now what else do you need help with?"

Trin shook her head and smiled. "Nothing. Just pour us another drink and have a seat. This will be ready in no time."

Kit did as she was told, which meant her pain must be more than she was letting on. Trin continued to prepare their meal, enjoying her sister's company as she did.

"So, tell me. What's going on with the handsome Officer Hardy?" Kit asked.

"Nothing at the moment. He and Caris have been dealing with a few things of their own."

"Like what?" Kit tossed an olive into her mouth.

"Nothing I want to discuss." Trin winked. "He and Caris are great, but for some reason, I feel like I need to keep my distance for the time being. We'll see how things play out."

"But you like him, right?"

"Yes, Kit, I like him. But I'm in no rush to start a

relationship, especially when we're so close to finding Kara. The need to be with both my sisters is consuming me. We need our power back."

Chapter Fifteen

IPSWICH, MASSACHUSETTS
1693

Karina fell to the floor and wept, knowing she'd never see her beloved Jeremiah again. Soft sobs continue to drift from her as day turned to night, with only the sounds of rodents skittering across the stone floor disrupting her mournful cries.

The metal door rattled, shocking her awake. "On your feet, witch," spat the officer looming just beyond her cage. "It's time for you to burn."

Karina stood, smoothing her dress and gathering her wits. "I thought the proper way to dispatch a witch was by hanging her on Gallows Hill? Is that not our destination?"

"After what Danforth saw, you're headed straight to the flame."

Karina knew the answer before she asked the question, but any delay would give her more time to finalize a plan. Kara and Kenna had both spoken to her using their minds, pleading that she let them come save her, but she'd refused. She would not have them face the same fate and would use every ounce of her magic to ensure it. She just wasn't sure how yet.

Bound once again, Karina was dragged through the prison and into the courtyard. The waiting crowd hissed and cursed hatefulness upon her as she was led to the stake.

Once tied in place, the pomp and circumstance began.

"Hear ye, hear ye. We gather this night to present evidence of solid conviction upon this witch, Karina Howe. Her use of dark magic was witnessed by our own Governor Danforth, and the accusing Ann Putnam."

Karina found Mrs. Putnam clinging to her baby at the front of the crowd. She quickly scoured the other faces, looking for her friend, Sarah Bishop, to no avail. The fact that she was nowhere to be seen, did not bode well.

"The devil's mark has been identified upon her and as the Court declares, 'Thou shalt not suffer a witch to live.'"

With no further words, the torch was cast at her feet. Karina was out of time. The crowd roared like zealots, cheering and excited for her death, but fell quiet when she smiled and opened herself up to the full well of magic she carried within.

Flames licked the hem of her dress as she worked to free her hands from the ropes. Somber faces, etched with malice or fear, looked on as she squirmed against the stake. She refused to close her eyes or scream. She wouldn't give them that. No. She would prove to be as defiant and wild as they deemed her while dragging her from her home.

Kara and Kenna stood hidden at the back of the crowd, silently pleading for her to use her magic to escape. She wanted to, oh how she wanted to, just to see these *Puritans* running for the hills. But staring into her sister's eyes as her legs started to burn, she knew she had to do whatever it took to keep them safe.

She closed her eyes, the chant beginning simple as always, words from the Goddess flowing into her mind. "*Come to me, death that be, flames surrounds, peace abounds; flesh to earth, spirit to soar, transport our souls, alive forever more.*"

Bursting free of her mortal flesh, Karina's soul flew into the cosmos. Encased in fire and wind, her energy signature spun wildly into the night sky. She could feel traces of magic sparking against her own and knew her spell had worked. Though divided by space and time, she and her sisters had escaped that horrible life and would return to the world, safe and sound when the time was right.

"You aren't still holding onto the notion that Caris is the one we're looking for, are you?" Kit asked.

"No. You were right. If it was her then Jason wouldn't even be part of her life, and after all the time I've spent with her, there would have been some kind of revelation I would think, like when I always find you."

Kit smiled. "Yes, there's never been any doubt for me either."

Trin placed the dish of chicken parmesan on the island and thought back to the first time she and Kenna met in their new lives.

It was 1785, almost a full century in the future, though it felt as if no time had passed at all. Karina's energy was fused into a nurse who was at the bedside of John Hancock when he resigned as Governor of Massachusetts due to his failing health. Karina had full memory of her previous life, as well as the one she'd just inherited. Her name was now Caroline Hughey, and though her magic was weakened, she could still feel it coursing through her veins.

Caroline wasn't married and lived a modest life, one that Karina slipped into with comfortable ease. Every night she would use her magic to scry for her sisters, knowing her powers wouldn't fully return until they were reunited.

Three months into her new life, Caroline was treating a young woman and received a massive shock upon touching her skin. A bright red energy burst forth, surrounding the girls. It was the young woman who spoke first.

"It's you. I've finally found you."

Karina cast a silencing spell upon the room so the two of them could speak freely. Karina recognized the magic within the woman and from that day forward, they lived together, searching for their sibling until their time to pass was upon them.

The same cycle had now repeated for nearly four centuries. Always finding one another, but never the third. Trin, however, was convinced and determined their curse was coming to an end this time around.

"Dinner was delicious," Kit complimented, snapping Trin from her thoughts.

"Thank you. Now why don't you head to bed. I'll clean up here."

Kit smiled and retreated up the stairs, leaving Trin to fantasize about how wonderful it would be to once again have both her sisters under her wing.

She hung the dish towel and walked onto the back porch to gaze at the night sky. "Lord and Lady, blessed be. Let this be the time of three. Reunited in spirit and soul, bring about the end of our goal."

A scream pierced the night. With panic rising in her chest, Trin raced inside and up the stairs to Kit's room. Throwing open the door, Trin quickly took in the scene and found Kit's injured hand surrounded by a thick twisting fog.

Trin blasted a spell into the room, striking the obscenity full on.

"Kit! My god, are you okay?"

Kit pulled her ravaged hand close to her chest, weeping as the wisps of fog disintegrated before her eyes.

"Talk to me. What happened?" Trin pleaded.

"I'm not sure." Kit sobbed. "I pulled up the covers and a pain exploded through my hand. When I sat up, there was this...darkness swirling around my wound." Kit threw herself into Trin's arms.

Trin held Kit as she cried, scared and unsure of what their next step should be. After a few minutes of contemplation, Trin swallowed and broke the silence.

"Kit, I think we should talk to Caris and Jason."

Kit leaned back and wiped her cheeks. "Do you really think they can help?"

"I do. I think that whatever this was, it's the same thing that attacked him." Trin opened the jar of salve on the nightstand and dabbed some ointment onto Kit's hand. "I think together we'd have a better chance at figuring out what it is."

Kit stared at her sister, unsure if opening their magic to outsiders was the best idea. Her concern wasn't purely selfish, but based on years of cause and effect. Trin was always thrown off when another witch was around. She so desperately wanted everyone they'd stumbled across to be Kara, that she'd lost perspective over the years. Her magic was wilder and unfocused, and it never ended well.

"If you think it's the right thing to do, then I'm okay with it." Kit sighed. "But you know me, Trin. I'm a private person and it's hard for me to open up to strangers. Especially about our magic. I think we're always stronger together—without outside influences."

Trin sat on the edge of the bed with her shoulders slumped.

"Okay, Kit. We'll search on our own if that's what you want. But if we come up blank, I'm asking for their help. Deal?"

Kit sniffled and brushed her nose with the back of her hand. "Deal."

Trin surrounded Kit's palm with her hands, concentrating on her wound and created a pulsing, healing light. "There. Now, does that feel better?"

"Yes, thanks to you. As always, you saved me." Kit's tears

returned in earnest.

Trin took her sister in her arms, hugging her tightly and giving thanks to the gods that she was okay.

Chapter Sixteen

"Are you sure you should go to work?" Caris asked.

"I feel fine, and yes, if we'd like to eat this month, I have to go to work," Jason teased.

"Please be careful, and promise you'll call me if anything happens."

"I will."

Jason kissed Caris on the cheek and headed for the station. Calling his cousin was a given, but calling Trin was the thought currently needling his mind.

They were meant to have a date in just over two days, but after everything that had happened, he hadn't heard hide nor hair from her.

After parking his squad car, he fiddled with his phone, debating whether it would be best to call early in the morning, or wait until late afternoon. "Stop acting like a girl, and just do it you pussy," he scolded himself.

Punching the contacts button, he scrolled to Trin's entry and hit CALL before he chickened out.

"Hello?" Her voice was thick and groggy. Sexy.

"Hi. It's Jason. Did I wake you?"

"Hi. Um, yeah...we had a long night."

Jason's ears perked up. "Everything okay?"

The line went silent.

"Trin? Are you and Kit okay?"

After another brief hesitation Trin sighed. "Yes. We're fine."

He could sense her lie straight through the phone.

"Are you sure?"

"Yes, I'm sure. How are you doing? Anything else going on over there?"

Even from this distance he could tell she was pushing him away. "No. Nothing else. I was just calling to see if we were still on for the weekend."

"The weekend? I only thought we were having dinner Friday night."

Jason closed his eyes. He could sense she was happy about their date, even though she was purposely trying to keep him at arm's length. Something was up, and he needed to understand what.

Taking a deep breath, he cleared his mind and opened his third eye to focus on Trin. The vision came quick and sharp.

Trin was surrounded by the same black fog that had attacked him. The only difference, it wasn't hurting her, but simply hovering around her aura, sucking and siphoning off bits and pieces.

"Well, I hoped we could start off with dinner Friday night, and thought maybe we'd try our hand at a road trip and venture to the falls on Saturday."

He held his vision and hoped his words would elicit a change.

"Niagara Falls?"

"That's the one."

Trin's aura spiked, a kaleidoscope of colors: pink, yellow, blue, and red, all mixed and pulsed with her magic, revealing her obvious excitement. Jason held his response for a split second while he watched the fog-ling sink multiple tendrils into Trin. Her colors diminished slowly as the cloud fed and pulsed.

"But if you're not feeling up to it, just let me know." Jason closed his third eye, unable to watch any longer.

Trin held her tongue as she fought the tug-of-war between her heart and head.

"I'm sorry, Jason. But as wonderful as that sounds, I'm going to have to pass. Kit just got back in town and we have some things around the house that need attending to."

Jason could feel her disappointment about canceling their date, and her regret for lying to him.

"No problem, Trin. I'll catch up with you later. Let me know if there's anything around the house that I could help with. I'm pretty good with a hammer and would love to see you."

"Thanks, Jason. I will."

Jason ended the call and immediately threw the phone across the car and onto the floor, scrambling to retrieve it when it started ringing again.

"Hello. Trin?"

"Um, no. It's me. What's wrong?" Caris replied.

"What do you mean?"

"I mean...I could feel your anger and anxiety and want to know what's going on?"

"I can't talk about it now. I have to get on the clock. I'll see you at home and we'll discuss it then."

Jason stowed his phone in the deep pocket on the front of his vest and entered the station. He hoped the day-to-day routine of protecting people would be a fulfilling distraction to the chaos in his private life.

"Bonds are torn, wounds are formed. Breaking trust, squashing lust. Separate will they ever be. This I swear, so mote it be." He tossed the chard bone and rats tail into the fire as the words sizzled in his mouth. His last spell had worked, fulfilling his targeted purpose perfectly and strengthening him in the process, but this last hit had drained him more than he cared to admit. He was determined to be successful again in this century, just as he had in the past three, but he needed more power. Thankfully, he knew exactly how to get it.

Trin threw back the covers and stomped into the shower. Having to lie to Jason and miss out on a great weekend because of all this crap had not left her in a very good mood. She wanted to get to the bottom of this and move on with her life, and after she was showered, fed, and brought Kit up to speed, that was precisely what she was going to do.

Trin sat in the kitchen, enjoying her preferred cinnamon and spice oatmeal, and waited for Kit to wake. After last night's drama, she needed as much sleep as possible.

Trin placed her bowl in the sink and felt the buzz of her cell going off in her pocket.

"Hello."

"Hi Trin, it's Mia. We need you to come in today. Say, in about an hour?"

Trin sighed. She'd placed herself on call after missing the couple of days she'd set aside for her trip to Ipswich. "Of course."

Trin didn't bother waking Kit. She knew she'd text her later, wondering where she was once she was up and about. Trin finished dressing then headed straight for work. "If it's not one thing delaying us it's another," she confessed to herself.

"Thanks for coming in, Trin. We've got a few extra bookings that we just couldn't shift around," Mia explained.

"It's no problem."

Trin resolved herself to an afternoon of work, happy to have a secure job in this unsecure economy. She'd answered Kit's text about her whereabouts around noon, and was now greeting her next client of the day. As she struggled past the thought that she'd rather be working magic with her sister than kneading Mr. Clemens' back folds, a wave of dizziness hit her, accompanied by a sudden case of nausea that sent her fleeing from the room.

"Trin...are you all right?" Mia asked from outside the bathroom stall.

"I'm sorry, Mia, but no, I'm not feeling well at all. Could you please give my apologies to Mr. Clemens and reschedule him for a free hour sometime next week?"

"Sure. No problem."

Trin hovered over the toilet in fear of losing her lunch. She had no idea what was happening but tried to take a few deep breaths to calm her stomach and nerves.

Once washed up, Trin gathered her things from the locker room and immediately returned home.

"You're home early. What happened?" Kit asked from her perch at the dining room table. She had papers and sketch books spread across the entire area.

"I don't know. One minute I was fine and the next I was on my knees in the bathroom feeling sicker than a dog."

Kit jumped up from the table and laid a hand across Trin's forehead and stomach. Closing her eyes, she drew upon her magic to weed out the cause of Trin's state of ill-being, like her sister had done for her so many times before.

A few seconds later Kit declared, "I don't see anything magical going on. Do you think you could have eaten something that didn't agree with you?"

Trin sagged into one of the dining room chairs. "I suppose so. But with everything that's been happening around here, I just assumed it was due to whatever 'evil' is attacking us." Trin dropped her head to the table while Kit set to making them both a cup of ginger tea.

"Here, drink this. It should help."

Trin lifted her head and took a sip, thankful to be waited on for once. Kit continued to hover about as Trin took a few more swallows. Stressed and tired, Trin tried to relax but was sent into a full-blown panic when she began to cough up blood.

Chapter Seventeen

"Oh my god, Trin. Here. Hold still." Kit handed Trin a napkin and tossed the remaining cup of tea down the sink.

"Thanks." Trin sputtered into the tissue, then wiped the spittle from her lips. "Are you still convinced this wasn't magically induced? Why would ginger make me cough up blood?"

"I'm not sure. But I don't think we should jump to conclusions. Maybe you should see an actual doctor first. What if you're having some intestinal issues that can be easily treated?"

Trin pushed back from the table and fetched herself a glass of water. No matter what Trin thought was going on, Kit disagreed. It was infuriating, especially when the damn fog-thingy had just attacked her one night prior. It wasn't like she was making this shit up.

"Fine. I'll go to the doctor, but only after you agree to do a spell with me. We need to find out about this shadow thing and see what the connection is with Jason and Caris."

Kit stood, uncommitted for what felt like an eternity, then finally nodded in agreement. "Okay. Let me finish up with my work here, then we'll head downstairs and see what we can find out together."

Trin nodded and headed for the stairs. "I'm going to rest for a while. Come get me when you're ready to begin."

Kit smiled and returned to her papers, putting the last touches on her sketches and drafting up her summaries and proposals. She needed to focus on real life and make sure her next showing was as successful as her last. Maybe once she knew the bills would continue to be paid, she could then worry about the impending evil that had come to town. Ironic nothing like this had happened before the Hardy's arrival. "Ironic, indeed," Kit spat.

She worked in silence, upset at the thought of Trin hurt in any way. Was it so bad that all she wanted was to remain sheltered and protected with her? They'd spent centuries together, safe and sound, and it was a life she enjoyed. Kit had no need of false covens or Wiccan friends. She had all she needed with Trin, and at times, it hurt that she didn't feel the same.

"Caris, I'll be home at six. We've got a lot to discuss, so order in some food, okay?"

Caris noted the tension in Jason's tone even through the voicemail. She texted back her reply to his message immediately.

Caris: *"I'll have dinner ordered and on the table by six. See you soon."*

Jason: *"Thanks."*

Caris called in their pizza order and headed straight to the shed. She was certain Jason would want to work a spell tonight, the tingle of magic along her veins was a tell-tale sign.

In just under thirty minutes she had their altar set up and returned to the house to pay for their meal and welcome her cousin home.

"How was work?" she asked, not quite sure if he'd be ready to dive straight in.

"Work was fine." Jason grabbed a slice of pepperoni and took a seat at the kitchen island.

"No more attacks from the evil bank of fog?" Caris

smiled.

Jason shook his head. "No. Not on me, anyway."

"What does that mean? Who else has been attacked?" Caris was in his face, demanding to know more.

"That's the thing...I saw the fog-ling surrounding Trin's aura, but it wasn't attacking her. It seemed like it was feeding off her."

Caris's hand flew to cover her mouth.

"Yeah. Not great news," Jason summarized. "We have to find out what this thing is and where it came from. I get that Trin is the most powerful witch around, but if it's feeding off her, then why would it have attacked me instead of doing the same, if magic is what it wants?"

"I don't know, none of the other attacks we've faced over the centuries compare to this. It's starting to freak me out." Caris paused then looked back at her cousin. "And how on earth did you even see this, anyway? I thought you were at work all day."

"I was. But when I called Trin this morning to confirm our weekend plans, she cancelled and lied to me. I could feel there was something off, so I used my third eye to gaze upon her, and that's when I saw it. It's like she doesn't even know it's there."

"Well, finish that damn slice and let's get to it. I can't stand sitting here not knowing what's going on, waiting for the next shoe to drop."

"I agree." Jason shoved the last bite of pizza in his mouth and grabbed a beer from the fridge.

They walked towards the shed, ready to connect their magic and search for the root of their problems. Suddenly a howling wind pierced the night sky, blowing around them in a vortex of tornadic proportions. Debris flew into the air, slamming violently all around them.

"What the hell is this?" Caris yelled.

"I think we're being blocked," Jason shouted, covering his head to avoid the flying clay planter coming his way.

"Come on! Let's get back inside." Caris clapped her hands in front of her, shoving them like an arrow through the deluge of rain.

Jason grinned at her display of water magic as they walked through what felt like the parted Red Sea. They trudged to the back door, slamming the screen once safely inside and continued to watch as wind and hail assaulted their backyard. Within minutes, their shed had collapsed, and the entire lawn looked like a warzone.

"Looks like you're right. Whatever is causing all this, certainly doesn't want us poking around," Caris said.

"Well, that's too damn bad," Jason swore. "This thing has its hooks in Trin, and I refuse to be scared into doing nothing."

"I have the tooth from Lillian, remember. But we need to

use it on the new moon, and that's not for another week."

"We'll bide our time while we restock and set up an altar in here," Jason confirmed.

"I have a few things in the kitchen already, let's do a quick protection spell and see if it helps."

Caris gathered the ingredients from her small stock and cast a quick circle, then grabbed Jason's hands and chanted her spell. "Goddess of love, goddess of light, protect us with your awesome might. Within this bubble we are safe, protected by your loving grace."

A churning silver bubble radiated from the two of them, encompassing the entire house and surrounding area. The wind stopped, and the hail ceased, immediately returning peace to their space. Caris and Jason ran to the backdoor and watched as a thick gray fog slithered back into the forest.

Chapter Eighteen

His breath came in short bursts as he summoned a fire to quickly bring the contents in his cauldron to a boil. He added a dash of his own skin and waited until the mixture turned pure black, then ran his long fingernail through the potion. Smearing his chest with the thick liquid, he chanted, "Forever one, so are we, bound by time, eternally. I will not lose you, our bond is true. Forged by magic, through and through." His chest sizzled, and the black smear disappeared into his flesh.

Trin woke what felt like days later, but with a quick glance at the clock, she realized it had only been three hours. Padding down the stairs in her flannel pj's and slippers, she wondered why Kit hadn't come to wake her up before now.

A quick glance at the dining room table brought up another question. Kit's papers were still scattered all over. Where the heck was she?

"Kit. Are you here?"

Trin knew it shouldn't have taken her this long to finish her proposals, as she'd seen her do it a dozen times before. Receiving no response, Trin thought perhaps her sister had started the spell without her, not wanting to disturb her sleep. She opened the door to the cellar and called out. "Kit. Are you down there?"

Again...no response.

Panicked and now fully awake, Trin began to scour the house.

There were no signs of a struggle and all the doors and windows were shut and locked. All but the front. It stood slightly ajar, letting in a chilled breeze, one that scattered a light dusting of snow over the threshold. Trin shivered as terror filled her veins.

She slammed the door, locked it, and ran into the cellar. Gathering her scrying mirror, Trin tossed a flame at the candles on the altar and set to finding out what the hell had happened while she'd been asleep.

The mirror swirled and the vision came quick. Kit was sitting at the table when suddenly, the front door burst open. Kit walked out onto the stoop, peering left and right, then turned back towards the house. Suddenly, the door slammed shut then rebounded slightly. Through the crack of the opening, Trin could see that Kit was nowhere in sight.

"Dammit!"

Trin quickly gathered a map and her pendulum for a locator spell. Pulling deep on her magic she demanded, "Show me my sister." The crystal point spun wildly, vibrating between multiple spots. Their house, the Hardy's, the forest, Washington DC, Ipswich and various routes in-between.

"What the hell?" Trin cussed.

Raising the bar, Trin nicked her thumb on the ceremonial knife she'd purchased from Lillian's shop, and placed a drop of blood on the tip of the pendulum. "Show me my blood sister."

Trin gasped as the crystal point stilled then shifted between only two spots on the map. The Hardy's house, and Washington DC.

"Hey. You started without me?" Kit's voice came from the bottom of the stairs.

Trin dropped the pendulum and spun around. "What the hell happened to you?"

"What are you talking about? I just ran to the store." Kit

frowned, holding up a bag of candles and a container of salt. "I thought we could use these for the spell and last time I checked, we were running low."

"But..." Trin looked back at her tools on the altar and took a deep breath. "I came downstairs and all your papers were still scattered across the table and the front door was open. I thought something happened to you."

"Really? The front door was open?"

"Yes. Really."

Trin stared at Kit, her anger and suspicion continuing to rise. Why wouldn't Kit tell her what happened? Trin turned to clear her things without another word, figuring she too could play it close to the vest and perhaps find out exactly what Kit was hiding in the process.

Kit walked to the altar and made quick work of setting up the candles she'd just purchased. She could tell Trin was still upset. "I'm sorry I worried you. The door must have blown open again after I left."

Trin huffed. "What do you mean again?" she prodded, failing to appear disinterested.

"I was sitting at the table and the door just blew open. I went to check it out, but nothing was there. The wind was blowing like crazy though, so I thought if I was going to run to the store I'd better do it then, instead of later in case the weather continued to worsen. So, I shut the door and ran to the store. I already had my keys in my pocket and my wallet was still in the car."

Trin stared at her sister as she processed her words. It was a *somewhat* logical explanation, and as Trin thought back she reminded herself that there weren't any signs of a struggle. She closed her eyes and shook her head. "I guess my imagination is getting the best of me these days. I'm glad you're okay."

Kit smiled and poured a circle of salt around the altar. "Don't worry, Trin. Nothing is going to happen to me. I've got you watching my back."

Trin forced a grin onto her face and glanced again at the pendulum she'd placed back on the shelf. *But who is truly watching my back?* she thought to herself.

Chapter Nineteen

Focused on their goal, Trin and Kit cast another locator spell to find their lost sister. The result was the same as always, no luck. They had tried scrying, vision work, pendulums, and like every time before, nothing had pinpointed a location or person. It was beyond depressing.

"Dammit!" Trin cussed.

"I'm sorry, Trin. We'll keep trying. The new moon is only a week away and maybe it's that energy we need to boost our spell," Kit offered.

"Possibly. We've always centered our magic around the full moon, so maybe you're right, it might just be that our timing is off." Trin shrugged a shoulder.

"If we don't get any results then, we'll plan a trip to Ipswich and speak to the shopkeeper you told me about. Okay?"

"Okay, Kit. Thanks."

The girls worked in silence, clearing and cleansing the space. Trin then returned to her room, ready to call it a night. Placing her long auburn hair in a high bun, she washed her face then headed straight for bed. She nestled under the thick duvet only to notice the light flashing on her cell phone. Trin reached to retrieve the message.

"Trin, it's Caris. We had another attack tonight. I really think it would be in everyone's best interest if we could combine our power and try to get to the bottom of this. Please call me back as soon as you get this."

Trin covered her eyes with her forearm and sank into the pillows. She hated the idea of anything bad happening to Caris or Jason and felt the urge to dial her back right away, but something stopped her. Trin couldn't tell if it was magic or the Goddess's subtle warnings, but she couldn't deny the feeling of wanting to keep her distance and honor Kit's wishes. Trin wiped a tear from the corner of her eye and replaced her phone on the nightstand.

She'd call Caris in the morning.

"Just so you know, I left Trin a message last night. I really think you need to tell her everything you saw," Caris stated flatly as she handed Jason his cup of coffee.

"Well, it's not that I don't agree, but without confirmation I'm not sure she'll believe a word I have to say."

"Then we need to figure out a way to give her some confirmation."

"Easier said than done, cousin. Easier said than done," Jason said as he headed out the door. "Text me when she calls."

"Will do." Caris finished packing her lunch and was climbing into her Jeep when her phone beeped. She looked at the display and grinned. "Morning, Trin. How are you?"

"Honestly, Caris, I've been better." Trin sighed.

"Same here." Caris huffed. "Did you get my message? Will you be able to come over tonight?"

"Yes, as long as I don't get sick at work again," Trin explained.

"Oh no. Are you okay?"

"Yes. I'm fine. I'll share all the gory details later. I'll text you once I'm on my way."

"Okay, great! See you later."

"See ya."

Caris hung up the phone and texted Jason before pulling

out of the drive.

Caris: *Trin will be over tonight.*

Jason: *Good. I'll try to get out early.*

Caris: *Sounds like a plan. Work on that confirmation. lol.*

Jason: *Ha ha. You too.*

Caris headed to work with her heart a little lighter. If they could convince Trin that she was the center of whatever it was that was happening around them, maybe then she would use her true magic and set Caris's free in the process.

Trin worked a full day with no debilitating illnesses wreaking havoc on her insides and was now heading out to meet Caris and Jason.

Trin: *We still on?*

Caris: *Yep. See you soon.*

Trin shook her head, still not convinced whether this was a good idea or not. As she rounded the corner onto the 9N, her phone rang.

"Hello?"

"Hey, where are you?" Kit asked.

"Oh, sorry, I was completely booked today and forgot to mention that I had plans after work."

"What kind of plans? Anything I can help with?"

"Nah. I'm just heading over to see Jason and Caris for a bit." Trin tried to keep it light.

"Oh." Kit's tone turned glacial. "I guess I'll see you when you get home, then."

Trin sighed. "Do you want me to pick up dinner? I shouldn't be long."

"Sure. Whatever you want," Kit snapped.

Trin rolled her eyes. "See you soon, Kit."

The line went dead.

Trin was used to her little sister never liking when she found new friends, but after centuries together, her jealousy was getting old. It was always like this; one minute she was promising to do everything in her power to find Kara, and the next, she was acting as if they should be sitting on their hands, not doing a damn thing. And the funny thing was, tonight wasn't even about Kara, it was about what happened to Jason and Caris, and to Kit as well. They needed to find a way to stop this mutual enemy, so Kit was just gonna have to suck it up.

Trin pulled up to the Hardy's place, again awestruck at their little slice of heaven. She loved this house and felt at peace within its walls.

"Thanks for having me over," Trin said, "I only wish it was under better circumstances."

"Me too. We have a lot to tell you, Trin. Hopefully Jason

will be here soon." Caris looked at her watch.

"How about a drink while we wait," Trin suggested, hoping to ease the increasing tension.

"Yes. Absolutely." Caris grabbed two on-the-rocks glasses and filled them both with a dash of bourbon.

"How's work?" Trin asked.

"It's great. I absolutely love this school and all my students are a real joy. Well, except for Katherine. That child..." Caris cut off, shaking her head.

"There's always one." Trin smiled.

"Ain't that the truth?" Caris laughed, relaxing them both.

The next twenty minutes flew by, filled with girl talk and shopping lists. Finally, Caris took another glance at her watch and picked up her cell to leave a message. "Jason, where are you? Trin is here, and I thought you said you'd try to get off early. Call me."

"If we need to do this some other time, I can come back," Trin offered.

"No, no. Jason and I really need to talk to you, and he should have been here by now. I'm sure he'll be strolling in any minute."

"Okay." Trin sipped at her drink and questioned why Caris couldn't broach the subject herself. She watched as Caris fiddled about the kitchen and realized this was her way of dealing with stress, but when she actually started putting dinner together, Trin decided it was time to cut to the chase. "So, were either of you hurt in the attack?" she asked, setting her glass on the counter.

Caris shoulders dropped as she turned from the stove. "No. Thankfully."

"Why can't you tell me what happened?"

"Because, Trin. There's so much more to it than just the attack last night."

"Like what? What does this have to do with me?" Trin stood and paced the kitchen.

"Please, let's just wait for Jason," Caris pleaded.

"Actually. I can't. I told Kit I wouldn't be long, and I still need to pick up dinner. Tell your cousin we'll have to reschedule."

Trin gathered her coat and purse and headed for the front door. "Sorry, Caris. Just let me know when it's convenient for me to come back."

Caris's response was interrupted by the ringing of her phone. "Wait, Trin. It's Jason." "Hello? Jason. Where are you?"

Trin's heart sank as all the color faded from Caris's face.

Chapter Twenty

Caris fell to the floor, dropping her cell beside her. Trin raced to retrieve the phone, putting it to her ear.

"Do you hear me, you meddling witch? I'll kill him if you don't leave Trin alone," said a gruff voice.

"Who the hell is this?" Trin demanded.

The line went dead, filling the house with only Caris's sobs.

"Now do you wonder what this has to do with you? It's all about you!" Caris yelled.

Affronted, Trin jerked back. "Excuse me? How is any of this my fault? Nothing like this has *ever* happened to me before. Not until you and Jason came to town." Trin handed Caris back her phone.

"Are you kidding me? You think this is all *our* fault?" Caris pushed to her feet. "Jason used his third eye yesterday to catch a glimpse of you when he could feel something was off during your conversation. What he saw was that your aura has been surrounded by a thick fog that is feeding off you and siphoning your magic. All of what's happened—the lake, the attack on Jason, the assault on our workspace—it's all been about you. Something is trying to keep us apart, Trin. Can't you see that?" She waved her cell in Trin's face. "A lunatic just said he'd kill Jason if we don't stay away from *you*. I think that's a pretty clear indication of your involvement."

Trin gasped, her eyes filling with tears. "Then by all means...stay away from me." Trin grabbed her belongings from where they fell to the floor and bolted out the door.

Slamming her keys into the ignition, Trin raced down the long driveway, stopping the car when she reached the end. She was literally at a fork in the road. Trin let go of the tight reign she had on her emotions and cried until all her tears had been shed. Her first instinct was to run home and seek comfort with her sister, but then again, dealing with Kit's *'I told you so'* attitude wasn't something Trin could face at the moment. She thought about turning around and offering an apology and her assistance in finding Jason, but that, too, seemed like a mistake based on this recent threat.

Trin took a deep breath and grabbed her phone, dialing the Wellness Center. "Mia. It's Trin. Please clear my schedule for the next four days. I'll return on Monday. Thanks."

Trin tossed her phone onto the passenger seat and turned south towards Ipswich. It was time she got some answers on her own.

He glared at the boy, bound and gagged. A boy was all he'd ever be to him. He could kill him right now, but tempered the thought, deciding to use him instead. "You will all learn your lesson," he spat, throwing a chunk of hair into the flame. "Darkest hearts, darkest night, crush his thoughts of fancies flight. Turn from one, turn from all, stripped away your destiny will fall."

Caris returned to the kitchen to finish a dinner no one would eat. Slamming pots and pans into the sink, she used the familiar motion to scrub away some of her frustration. Drying her hands, she picked up her phone. "We need you. Please come home," Caris begged. The beep of the machine signaled the end of her message.

She was alone and struggling to figure out what she needed to do next. If distancing herself from Trin was the answer to getting Jason back, she was willing to do it. But every time she considered the thought, something nasty churned in her gut.

Chapter Twenty-One

Trin's journey was peaceful until her phone started to buzz an hour-and-a-half later.

"Where are you?" Kit demanded. "I thought you were bringing dinner home."

"Change of plans. There's some leftovers in the fridge and a casserole you can heat up in the freezer. That should get you by. I'll be home in a few days."

"What? Trin, what the hell are you talking about?"

"Kit. Please. I need some time alone, okay? I'll be back soon." Trin hung up the phone, refusing to argue or explain herself further.

Trin needed this, this time and space to clear her head and

hopefully get some help in deciphering what was happening to her. The more she thought about what Caris had said, the angrier she got. Trin couldn't deny the thorn of truth she felt within her words. She had always been able to draw on her magic, but never at the same level as before. She assumed it was part of her soul's journey, that her full powers would only return once she had reunited with both her sisters, but what if it was something else? What if something *had* been draining her in every lifetime between then and now?

She shook her head, not wanting to be weighed down with such depressing thoughts as she focused on the road.

Four hours later she was once again in a room at the Inn at Castle Hill. The quiet peacefulness within its walls was something she realized she'd been missing for quite some time.

BOSTON, MASSECHUSETTS
1898

"Excuse me, doctor, here are my papers."

Karina, now Kristine, turned to the man in the navel uniform and offered her assistance. She'd vaccinated all one hundred and ninety-two passengers of the SS Portland over the last few days.

"There you go, Officer Harris, no smallpox for you."

"Thank you, ma'am." The handsome seaman shook her hand, sending a lightning charge through her fingertips.

"Ouch. Please forgive me." Officer Harris rubbed his hands on his pants.

"No harm done." Kristine smiled, feeling a strange sense of connection. "Good voyage to you, sir. I hear Cape Cod is beautiful."

"Thank you, ma'am. Perhaps I'll return with a few pictures to share."

"That sounds lovely." Kristine blushed as the officer winked and left the room.

"Well, that was awkward," teased Camille, her assistant and soul sister.

This time around, they'd found one another after only two weeks into their new lives.

Kristine wiped down the tray and placed her needle back in the sterilization liquid. "I can't help it. I felt a strange connection with that man, and the shock his touch elicited sent a spark racing through my veins. I think he holds magic within him."

Camille sucked in a breath. "Really? We've never ran across anyone else magical before. How exciting."

Later than night, Kristine wept when the report came across the radio that the SS Portland had sank off Cape Ann. There were no survivors.

Trin woke with wet cheeks and more memories she'd need to reconsider. What if every time she'd encountered a magical person in the past, something had kept them apart and she'd been oblivious to it all?

Trin dressed and enjoyed the breakfast put on by the Inn, then drove straight to Lillian's shop, ready to find some real answers.

"Trin! How lovely to see you again." Lillian beamed.

Trin looked around the shop, making sure no customers were inside. "Lillian. I need a favor. Would you be willing to close down for a bit and help me find some answers to the strange things that have been happening lately?"

Lillian crossed to lock the door without another word. "Come, come. Let's sit and you can tell me what's been going on since your last visit."

"Thank you, but I have to be honest. I'm still skeptical about all this, but at this point, I'd simply be grateful for your help."

Lillian patted her hand. "I'm sorry if the story of our history shocked you. It wasn't my intent to upset you."

"It's okay. It's just a heavy burden to know that I single handedly ruined so many lives with one spell. I was only trying to save me and my sisters."

"Not all true witches retain the memory of our past, but for those of us who do remember, we're grateful you pulled us from that horrible place. Even though our powers are diminished here, without your spell, we certainly all would have died long ago." Lillian smiled kindly. "Now, tell me how I can help you."

Trin proceeded to explain everything, down to the final detail of Jason's disappearance.

Lillian took a deep breath. "I can't pretend to know what's really happening, but I can certainly help you find out." Lillian grasped Trin's hand and smiled as a charge passed between them. "Gather some charms that speak to you from around the shop, then join me in the back room," Lillian instructed.

By the time Trin placed a small pentacle, a silver triquetra, and a symbolized goddess pendant on the table, Lillian had laid out three cords and nine feathers atop the altar.

Trin stood silently while Lillian anointed the black and purple candles with rosemary oil for protection and magical powers.

"Trin, please put some mugwort in the censer," Lillian

asked.

Trin retrieved the herb from the neatly organized spice rack and set it alight in the incense burner.

"We're going to be making a witches ladder to help you climb into your past," Lillian announced. "The black cord represents the waning years, the white protection and purity, and the purple represents hidden mysteries coming to light. The black iridescent feathers will provide mystical insight, while the brown ones striped with black will bring balance between your physical and spiritual self. The blue feathers offer peace and protection as well as boosting your mental abilities and psychic awareness."

Trin took a deep breath.

"We'll place the eye of the peacock at the end, for it protects against the evil eye and stimulates clairvoyant visions," Lillian stated with an encouraging nod.

Trin stepped up to the altar, familiar with the process and began.

Securing a silver hoop to the hook on the side of the altar stand, Trin tied on each end of cord then started her braid.

"Yarn of black and purple and white, set this magic spell to flight."

Trin added the first feather into the ladder.

"With this feather and this string, awareness and answers this charm will bring."

Feeling the magic build with each cross-section, Trin continued to braid, adding in the feathers as she did. Trin tied the charms onto the end and placed the peacock feather firmly in place.

"In the names of the God and Goddess, I charge this charm of feathers nine and cord of three, as I will, so mote it be!"

Trin passed the witches ladder through the incense and flame, consecrating it, then handed it to Lillian, confident in her plan.

"I think it would be best if you lie down." Lillian led Trin to an intricately carved, oriental daybed that sat against the far wall.

"What should I do?" Trin asked, suddenly unsure of how to proceed.

"Ask the Goddess for answers and let the visions come." Lillian smiled as she coiled the ladder over Trin's heart.

Chapter Twenty-Two

Trin's mind was on fire, burning with centuries old images of witches hung from a tree on Gallows Hill, while others rotted in prison. The assault on her head and heart was almost too much to bear.

Trin felt Lillian's hand stroking her arm and gave thanks for her insight to use the brown and black feather to help focus her physical being. She took a deep breath and grounded herself in the present, becoming only a witness to the scenes playing out in her mind.

As she pulled back from the heartbreaking violence, she was able to see a thick fog coating the ground in the outlying areas of each image. Focusing her attention, she asked the

Goddess, *"My lady, with your keen insight, reveal the evil within."*

The ground slithered like a snake, parting the fog to show a horde of witches who'd been gnawed to the bone.

The image shifted, showing her and Kenna in their first life together after she'd cast her spell. A red cord of connection shone brightly, but a cloud of darkness had weaved its way into their bond. This repeated with each new life, the darkness thickening and their bond growing tighter with every reincarnation.

Trin woke, panicked that whatever was blocking her now had been doing the same to Kit for all these years.

Lillian looked drained and Trin quickly guided her to sit. "Were you able to witness any of my visions?"

"Only a few, but whatever is happening now, it's clear that it goes back to the casting of your original spell."

Trin sighed, feeling the weight of everything building within her. Not only was she responsible for scattering other witches throughout time, but apparently for bringing with them an evil that had woven its way into their lives.

"What can I do?"

"You have to find the source. It will be ancient and well-cloaked, but now that you have the thread, you can follow it to its core." Lillian handed Trin the witches ladder. "Keep this with you at all times, it will help reveal the truth."

Trin wrapped the cord around her wrist, holding the end as if it were a set of rosary beads. "Thank you, Lillian."

"You're welcome, but be patient, Trin, this may take some time. The magic you're dealing with is as old as we are." Lillian sighed.

Trin smiled as Lillian moved back to the front of the store, needing to open for the day's business. As Trin cleared the altar, she noticed the locked case off to her right. Peeking again at its contents, she realized the demon's tooth was missing.

"Lillian?" Trin called.

Trin heard the bell on the front door and walked out to pose her question privately. Gazing from left to right, Trin found no one in sight, including Lillian.

"Lillian, where are you?" Trin walked to the door, peering out the window. No one was there, but as Trin turned to move she caught sight of a thick black fog retreating from the sidewalk and into the sewer drain.

Trin spun around and ran to the heart of the store. Searching from side-to-side, Trin finally spotted Lillian on the floor behind the counter. Her life and magic had been completely drained.

Trin summoned all her magic and placed her hands above Lillian's heart. "Lord and Lady, please grant me a boon. Heal the wound of this faithful witch, for she does not deserve to die like this."

Trin's usual healing abilities sparked to life, but they weren't enough to save her friend. Trin dialed 911, then sat, crying until the paramedics arrived. They, too, were unable to resuscitate Lillian, which Trin already knew would be the case. The police on scene asked her all kinds of questions, which was no surprise. Searching a shop of this kind always prompted suspicion and fear. Luckily, Lillian was a pillar member of the community and most of the officers had known her personally. Five hours later, the next of kin had been contacted and Trin was free to go.

She returned to her room at the Inn and collapsed onto the bed. Tears continued to roll down her cheeks as she thought about Lillian. Trin rubbed the witches ladder between her thumb and finger and debated calling Caris. It was she, after all, who had introduced her to Lillian. But, recalling their fight, Trin decided against it. Caris had been right. Everything happening was her fault, and she refused to put anyone else in danger.

Trin cast her usual protection spell before crawling in to bed, then flicked her finger towards the light, casting the room into a quiet darkness.

Chapter Twenty-Three

He cut the rope, freeing the boy's hands and began preparing him for transport. His lifeless body would be found on the cold ground at the boundary of his woods. Oh, the pup would soon wake and make his way home, telling the tale of his capture, which is exactly what he wanted. He needed them scared, needed them to keep their distance or else he'd be forced to take more drastic measures.

Jason woke cold and sore, at the edge of a forest that ran along an unfamiliar road. Digging in his pocket with shaky hands, he found all his belongings, including his cell phone and quickly dialed Caris.

"Car. It's me. Yeah, yeah, I'm okay," he muttered. "Listen, I'm gonna turn on my location service so you can track my phone. I think I'm along highway 1, but can't be sure." Jason fumbled with the buttons on the screen, his fingers stiff and aching. "You got it? Okay, thanks. See ya soon."

Jason hung up to the sounds of Caris's joyful sobs. It would take her at least forty-five minutes to get to him, so he needed to warm up. The pain in his sides made gathering kindling and wood a daunting task, but once stacked, he tossed flames from his fingers and eased down beside the fire. Soon, he felt the circulation returning to his frozen hands and tried to process all that had happened.

Wednesday afternoon, after Caris confirmed Trin was coming over, Jason finished his reports and punched out early. He wanted to get to the local herb shop to replenish the stock that had been destroyed in the attack on their shed. After paying for his oils, herbs, candles, and sage, he crossed the parking lot, returning to his car.

As Jason unlocked the door and placed his bag in the seat, a sickening dizziness took hold of him. He woke up bound and gagged in a cave with a cloaked man hovering over him.

The man barely spoke as he worked at his altar —a large piece of petrified wood scattered with rough, old tools. When his potion was mixed he flicked his hand towards Jason, ripping his cell phone from his pocket. Obviously familiar with modern technology, he dialed Caris and made his threats.

Satisfaction sat upon his mangled mouth, for it was all Jason could see from beneath his hood. "You will all learn your lesson," he spat, throwing a chunk of hair into the flame, then muttered some spell. Jason felt the same overwhelming dizziness settle over him, and the next thing he knew, he awoke in the woods, alive but with a few good bumps and bruises.

Jason took a deep breath and tried to walk backwards through the memories again. He focused on every detail, every smell and sound, looking for a clue as to where, who, or why this was happening. Unfortunately, nothing stood out and the question remained...*Why didn't he kill me?*

Caris arrived within the hour with a thermos of hot chocolate and some extra blankets, which she handed him after wrapping him up in a massive hug.

"Thanks." Jason winced.

"What is it? I thought you said you were okay." Caris's voice quivered as she struggled to hold back unshed tears.

"Yes, Car. I'm okay, but I think the bastard got in a few good kicks while I was out." Jason held his ribs, sucking in a breath as he struggled to climb into the Jeep. "Besides that, the only thing he actually did to me was steal a chunk of my hair I think." Jason reached up to the nape of his neck, feeling for the uneven cut. "He cast a spell just before he freed me."

"Could you decipher the spell?"

"Not really, something about destiny, I think. He said that we'd all learn our lesson."

Caris gasped. "That doesn't sound good. Do you think we should prepare for another attack?"

Jason shifted uncomfortably and felt an irritation settling in his chest. "Maybe we should just move away from here and not look back," he snapped.

Caris slammed on the brakes. "Why would you say that after all we've been through?"

"Because, after all this time, we are still no closer to finding the answers we seek. I think it's time we face facts and let go of the hope that Trin's the one."

"I'm not so sure we should, Jason. Think about it. We've never been this close before and you yourself saw that she was blocked. I think if we can find a way to free her from that, we would all be able to see the truth of things. Trin's the key, though I'm not sure getting her help will be easy at this point."

Jason squinted at Caris, "Why would you say that? Did something happen while I was gone?"

Caris took a deep breath. "We kinda had a fight."

Jason clenched his jaw and turned towards the window. The stress of the ordeal was finally catching up to him. He was tired. Tired of searching and hoping, and tired of always being let down. Maybe it was time he left Caris behind too and followed his own path.

"Great. One more thing we'll have to sort out. Can you take me to the herbal shop? I have to get my car."

"Are you sure you can drive?"

"Yes," Jason snapped.

Caris guided the Jeep back onto the road and decided to give Jason some peace and quiet for the rest of the ride home.

"We're here." Caris nudged his shoulder.

Jason looked up and spotted his patrol car right where he'd left it. He kicked the blankets off his legs and climbed out of the Jeep. Glancing through the window, he found his bag of supplies still lying in the seat behind a locked door. Jason fiddled in his pockets, retrieving the keys. "I'll meet you at home."

Caris cast him a sad smile then eased her Jeep forward, taking a left out of the parking lot.

Jason sat in his patrol car and debated if he should follow Caris home or simply take a right and leave. It's not like they needed him. He wasn't part of the three. Slamming his hands against the wheel, he pulled up to the street and checked his mirrors. Catching his reflection in the rearview, he reached up to the spot where he was missing a chunk of hair and cursed. "Fuck!" Realization dawned, and Jason scolded himself for missing it. "He's spelled you into wanting to leave, stupid."

Jason reached into his bag, retrieving the sage and punched the cigarette lighter. Grabbing it once ready, he lit the smudge stick and cleansed his heart and mind. "In the name of the Lord and Lady, please remove any negative energies affecting me at this time." He took a deep breath and felt the threads of the spell leave his body, carried away by the healing smoke.

Clear of mind once again, he checked his car, making sure no talismans were left behind to play with his head, then he, too, pulled out and headed south towards home.

Jason rounded the corner at the end of the drive and sucked in a shocked breath. Parking in a rush, he carefully exited the car, nursing his ribs. "What are you doing here?"

"Caris called and said you were in trouble and that I needed to come home, and from the looks of you, it was none too soon."

"Well, I can't deny I'm glad to see you. Come on in." Jason responded. "How was your drive?"

"Not bad. It's only nine hours from Washington, DC to BlackBrook."

Chapter Twenty-Four

After an entire day of selfish wallowing, Trin decided it was time for her to return home. With Lillian's death, there was no one else she could talk to about her situation, except Caris, Jason, and Kit. She'd decided that regardless of their fight, she wanted to inform Caris of what happened to her friend in person, and not knowing if Jason was all right had been eating her up inside. Two more hours and she'd be at the Hardy's door. Trin hadn't bothered calling Kit; experience had taught her that dealing with her face-to-face was the best way to go.

Clear of mind and happy to be moving towards some sort of amends, Trin turned on the radio and cracked the window, letting the crisp end-of-winter air keep her awake. She passed the miles thinking about all the moments in her past where she'd encountered another witch, only to be distanced by some twist of fate. But now, after everything she'd discovered, Trin was sure fate had nothing to do with it.

Stopping at a convenience store, Trin filled up with gas and grabbed a bottle of water for the last leg of her trip. She debated, again, whether to call in advance, but decided against it in case they refused her. No. She'd deal with that after she got there and said her piece.

With only miles to go, Trin's veins buzzed with a nervous energy and magic. Strangely enough, she felt a positivity settle over her that she hadn't felt in a very long time. Perhaps her vision walking with Lillian had somehow unblocked her after all. Trin certainly hoped so as she turned the last curve of the road and parked behind an unfamiliar Range Rover.

Grabbing her witches ladder, Trin walked to the front door and knocked.

"Trin!' Caris's high-pitched greeting was a surprise.

"Hello, Caris. May I come in, I have some news I need to share with you," Trin stated in a somber voice.

"Um...sure. Yeah, um...can you give me a minute?" Caris shuffled nervously, hoping the healing work on Jason's ribs was done.

Trin cocked her head. "Okay, but is everything all right? Is Jason all right?" Trin glanced past Caris's shoulder.

"Car, who is it?" Jason's voice rang out.

Trin sighed when Caris smiled and led her straight to the kitchen.

"You're okay," Trin stated.

"Yes. I'm okay." Jason moved to Trin, giving her a gentle hug.

"We have company?" a voice sounded from the back door.

Caris took a deep breath. "Trin. I'd like you to meet my sister."

Trin froze. Here stood another striking red-head, whose magic was singing in her veins. Trin laughed internally at the sight before her; two sisters resembling her own staring at her from across the kitchen counter, her lost love smiling down at her with his arm around her shoulders, and all the while knowing none of it could be true. She was losing her mind.

"Hi! I'm Trin." She offered her hand, not sure at this point what to expect.

"It's nice to meet you." The woman smiled but didn't return the gesture.

Caris huffed and motioned to the living room. "Let's all take a seat, it seems we have a lot to discuss."

Trin sat across from the Hardy's on one of the two couches, clutching tightly to the witches ladder in her pocket. The collision of her past and present was no longer avoidable.

She had to tell them the truth, all of it, if they had any hope of making sense of this mess. "Unfortunately, I must insist that I go first. The news I have may alter what you'd like to share," Trin explained.

Caris nodded and took a seat beside her sister and Jason on the opposite couch.

"After what happened," Trin nodded at Jason, "I fled to Ipswich in search of answers. I met with Lillian and she helped me make this." Trin produced the ladder and laid it on the coffee table between them. "It's a witches ladder and it helped me climb into my past. What I saw there is that you were both right. I have been blocked by something." Trin nervously retrieved the talisman and held it tight within her hand. "But what you don't know, is that it's been happening for centuries."

The Hardy siblings gaped at each other, smiling wide.

Trin took a deep breath, ready to reveal her secret. "I was born in 1673 as Karina Howe. I had two sisters, Kara and Kenna. We were all *true* witches, like our mother before us. I was set to the flame in 1693 where I cast a spell that catapulted our souls forward through time."

Jason smiled encouragingly at Trin, while the sisters continued to look on, interested but reserved.

"In every life I've lived since, I've found one of my sisters but never the other." She motioned towards Caris. "When I first met you, I thought you were Kara, but as Kit explained, you couldn't be her, as all my sisters live their lives as only children, waiting until the three of us can be reunited."

Caris cast a weary look at Jason, who just shook his head and let Trin continue.

"Lillian was able to help me see that something had attached itself to me during the casting of my spell. A demon most likely, and that it's been blocking me from finding my final sibling all this time."

Trin took a shaky breath as tears filled her eyes. "While I'm so grateful for Lillian's help, I wish I'd never gone."

Caris reached for her hand, absorbing the severe jolt between them without a word. "Oh, Trin. What happened?"

"Whatever has been attacking you followed me." Trin sobbed. "Lillian is dead."

Caris sucked in sharp breath and sank back onto the couch.

"I'm so sorry, Caris. You were right. It is all my fault." Trin wrapped her arms around herself as her tears fell. "I'm sorry to you, too, Jason. It's my fault you were taken. Can either of you ever forgive me?" Trin pleaded.

Jason rose and took Trin in his arms, kissing the top of her head, "It's okay, Trin, it's not your fault. There's nothing to forgive." He continued to rock her while she cried herself out.

Caris was led to the kitchen by her sister, who tried to comfort her over the loss of her friend. Caris continued to listen to her soft whispers, but it was the ritual of grinding herbs, letting them steep, and breathing in the gentle aroma of the tea that helped sooth her soul.

Jason nodded to the girls over Trin's shoulders. "Would you like something to drink?"

Trin nodded, feeling like a fool that she'd laid all her cards on the table, so to speak. What if sharing her secret with the Hardy's—all of them, ended up being a huge mistake?

Jason held Trin's hand and told her what happened during his capture while they waited for the tea. "Besides a few sore ribs and another round of hypothermia, I promise, I'm perfectly fine." Jason winked.

"I can't tell you how happy that makes me," she confessed, laying her forehead to his.

Suddenly, as if cast backwards through time, Karina and Jeremiah laid tangled in the sheets of their old bed. Kissing, fondling, and madly in love.

"Whoa...what was that?" Jason pulled back.

"Oh my god, I'm sorry. I must be projecting my desire for you. That was a vision from my past life of me with my beloved, Jeremiah."

Jason rose from the couch and excused himself. "How about I check on the tea? I'll be right back."

Trin collapsed face first onto the couch. How embarrassing. She needed to get control of herself, because it seemed that opening these floodgates may have been an all or nothing kind of thing. She didn't want to confuse the situation, especially for herself. Sitting up, she shook out her arms and ran her fingers through her hair. She'd get it together, and hopefully with the Hardy's help, they'd put a stop to whatever this was so they could all move on with their lives.

Jason returned to the living room with a plate of cheese and crackers, followed by the girls who carried in an elaborate tea set upon an antique silver tray.

They all sat their items on the coffee table and retreated a few steps, staring at Trin in an awkward silence.

Trin scanned each of their faces and offered a quirky, "Thanks?"

As she reached for the kettle Trin gasped. "Oh my god!" She looked up into three smiling faces. "This was my mother's platter. How on earth...?"

Caris's sister stepped forward. "Let me properly introduce myself." She knelt directly in front of Trin. "My name is Kennedy, and it's finally nice to see you again, *sister*."

Chapter Twenty-Five

A massive explosion of blue energy filled the entire room when Kennedy touched Trin's hand. It pulsed with a magic that only grew stronger when Caris joined in.

"I don't understand," Trin confessed. "This can't be possible."

"Trin. I really need you to listen to us, okay? We have a lot to tell you, and you're right, it's going to be hard to believe, but I promise you, we *are* your sisters," Caris stated.

Trin sat back on the couch, casting Jason a weary glance. She figured, however, if they could give her the courtesy of listening to her tall tale, the least she could do was offer them the same. "Okay. I'm listening."

Caris blew out a deep breath. "You have travelled through time thinking you've always found one sibling while still missing the other, when in reality, it's *you* who are the missing third. Kenna and I have always been together, along with Jeremiah." Caris cast a glance at Jason. "Your spell not only pulled us, your sisters, forward, but also any true witch in the vicinity at the time." She gestured to the three of them. "We've always been together, searching for you, not the other way around."

Trin gasped as her head wavered back and forth of its own accord. "How is that possible when I've *always* found Kenna? I recognized her energy just as I recognized the magic within you."

"You said it yourself earlier, Trin. Whatever has been blocking you attached itself to your soul at the time of the casting. It's been able to find you because you're intertwined, but it's not in the way you think," Kennedy stated.

"You've always felt it was Kenna you found, when in reality it was the demon who found you." Jason took her hand. "Kit isn't your sister, Trin. She's the bad guy," he summarized.

Trin pushed from the couch. "No! It can't be true! Kit has never hurt me," she snapped.

"Why would she? You're her meal ticket," Kennedy replied. "Why else do you think she attacked and threatened to kill Jason if we didn't keep away?"

Trin's heart was racing. "How can it be Kit when the thing doing this is a man?" Trin demanded.

"Trin, do you remember when Lillian told you about Henrich Kramer?" Caris asked.

"The demon who started the witch trials? Wait...how do you know what she told me?"

"Because, Lillian knew who I was and I asked her to fill you in. I thought it might help you to hear the story of our heritage, possibly jar your memories enough to knock loose whatever was blocking you." Caris continued with a sad smile. "Now, do you remember the part about the demon shapeshifting into a man?"

Trin's eyes grew big. "Are you saying this demon has transformed himself into a female for centuries, just to trick me?"

"I'm afraid so, sweetheart," Jason stated softly. "Think about your connection, is there any difference between what you see and feel with Kit, versus what you experience with us?"

Trin processed his words, focusing internally while she searched the memories of her recent vision walk. Unable to make it back to the couch, Trin fell to her knees and began to weep. "The connection I have with Kit displays as red and is mangled and twisted between us, while the energy we all share is pure blue and pulses with the Goddess's signature." Her heart wrenched as she looked up at Jason, Caris, and Kennedy.

"How could I have been so blind? I've spent life-time after life-time with this person, always hopeful we'd find the third, when all along, I was being duped."

Caris wrapped her arms around Trin while Kennedy poured everyone some tea. Jason grabbed Trin's hand and guided her back to the couch. "We need to figure out how to untangle you and Kit, because even though the three of you are now together, your powers are still being blocked."

Trin shook her head and wiped her tears. "Don't worry. I'll take care of that," Trin stated, remembering the reverse Tower card from her tarot reading. "Now that I know who I can and can't trust, it will be easy work to put up my own blocks while I try to break the connection."

"You'll have to get inside her, or *his* lair. Only at the source of his power will you be able to break the tie," Kennedy added.

"This is going to be tough, Trin. Will you be able to pretend nothing's changed until we find the cave?" Jason asked.

"I guess I'll have to," Trin said with a firm set to her jaw.

Chapter Twenty-Six

Trin had spent the rest of the night reminiscing with Caris, Kennedy, and Jason, each providing stories from the past that proved their claims. As the last spark from the fire cooled, Jason had held Trin in his arms and declared his undying love for his soul mate once again.

"Though you don't look the same, I feel you, Karina, deep within my soul. I've waited centuries for this moment, and I won't lose you again. We'll do whatever it takes to free you from this curse."

"Thank you, my love," Trin replied, *fully immersed in their relationship of old.*

Trin smiled at the memory of his lips on hers, and couldn't wait until his promise was fulfilled so they could be together in the here and now. But, at present, they all needed to keep their distance so Kit would assume her threats were continuing to work.

Trin: *On my way home. Need anything from the store?*

Trin wasn't sure what to say, but acting as if she had no idea that Kit had followed her to Ipswich and killed Lillian was going to be the greatest test of her acting abilities, not that she had any to begin with. She'd already asked herself, *"What would I normally do?"* over and over again. She had to continue to act like herself if they stood any chance at breaking this bond, when in reality, all she wanted to do was rip Kit limb from limb.

Kit: *No. I'm good. See you soon.*

It was obvious Kit was still mad at her for bolting out of town, but Trin also knew Kit wouldn't be able to stop herself from picking her brain about where she went and what happened. Trin was stuck. She couldn't lie about it, since Kit already knew the truth, so she was left trying to figure out a way to use that same information against her, maybe force Kit to slip up and reveal something she shouldn't.

Trin pulled into the drive, practically hyperventilating. She hated this, but knew it had to be done or all her newly found loved ones would remain at risk.

Despite Kit's response, Trin had grabbed some quick-heat lasagna from the store and a bottle of wine.

"Honey, I'm home," Trin mocked as she deposited the bags in the kitchen.

Kit sauntered down the steps and took a seat at the island. "So, are you going to tell me where you went and what prompted your spur of the moment get-away?" Kit had a smile on her face, but the tension in her words cut like a knife.

"I'm sorry. I was just getting really burned out at work, then with Jason wanting to take me to Niagara Falls for the weekend, and then my fight with Caris...everything was pushing in on me. I had to get away."

"You had a fight with Caris? Are you okay? What happened?"

Trin took a deep breath and prayed for the right words. "With the attacks that have been happening and Jason being abducted, she basically blamed me straight to my face."

Kit gasped. "You've got to be kidding? How can any of that be your fault? We've never faced any threat until those two came into your life. If you ask me...they're the ones who are the root of all our problems. We need to stay away from them, Trin."

"I agree." Trin turned to put the lasagna in the oven, hoping she was now off the hook.

"So where did you end up going?"

Trin's shoulders slumped. "Ipswich." She spun around. "I told you I wanted to go back and see Lillian, but that, too, was

a huge mistake. She had a heart-attack after meeting with me."
Trin covered her face with her hands and forced herself to cry.
"I don't know, Kit. Maybe I'm cursed and all this *is* my fault."

Kit walked to Trin and placed her hands on her shoulders.
"Don't you dare say such a thing. You are the kindest person I
know, and there's no way any of this is on you. Were you and
Lillian working on something stressful that could have caused
her heart to weaken? As you're well aware, all magic has a
price."

"No. She helped me do a bit of vision walking, but all it
revealed was *our* connection—throughout the centuries, and
that something has, in fact, been blocking us from finding
Kara."

"So you were right. Did she show you who or what is
blocking us?" Kit moved nervously to pour herself a glass of
wine.

"No. Just a strange fog, kinda like what Jason described,
and probably what attacked you the other night as well."

"Wow. I guess we need to put some more protections in
place before we continue searching for Kara." Kit paused.
"Hey, maybe it's all the magic you've been doing that's drawing
it to you. Do you think we should take a break for a bit, and see
if things die down?"

Trin grabbed a glass for herself from the cabinet. "Yeah.
That's probably a good idea. We've been waiting this long,

what's a few more months, I guess."

Kit smiled and took a sip of her wine, while Trin fortified the blocks she'd placed on her mind. If Kit could sense what she was truly thinking...dinner would not go well.

"Did you find anything?" Trin asked Caris in the private massage room of the Wellness Center. They'd decided this would be the safest place to talk and give them at least an hour or more to plot and plan without interference.

"No, not yet. Kennedy and I are a little stronger now that we're back together, but we're still nowhere close to full strength. Jason is taking a dog patrol up to where he was released, though, and hopefully they'll be able to track his scent back to the cave."

"Oh...that's a great idea. Wouldn't it be great if we could bring the demon down without using magic at all?" Trin snickered.

"Talk about irony," Caris laughed.

"Yeah, and a heavy dose of wishful thinking." Trin took a seat on the table and took a deep breath. "Caris, can I talk to you about Kennedy?"

"Of course. What would you like to know?"

"It's just that, I've spent hundreds of years with a person I thought was our little sister. Her thoughts and actions always matched the personality I associated with our Kenna from old. But now, with Kennedy here and our bond reforming, she isn't anything at all like I expected." Trin rushed to add, "Don't get me wrong, I'm beyond grateful to have found you both and definitely feel the love between us that we once shared, but it's a little hard to wrap my head around the fact that this bad-ass FBI agent is actually my little sister."

Caris laughed. "Yes, I can see how that would throw you off. But after you saved us, Kenna changed. She was so moved by the sacrifice you made to protect us, that it became her life's goal to do the same. Are you familiar with the Jim Crow laws of 1910?" Caris asked.

"Vaguely."

"Well, after they were imposed, the atrocities that came with such racial segregation were horrific. Kenna had already been developing her mental skills, but it was this particular turn of events that pushed her to work harder.

"By 1950, thanks to Kenna influencing public opinion, blacks had started moving into city neighborhoods that had previously kept them out." Caris smiled. "And the rest is history. Kenna has proven herself to be strong and selfless, just like you, in every life we've lived."

Tears pooled in Trin's eyes as pride overtook her. "I the

healer, you the teacher, and Kenna the protector. I can now clearly see the Goddess's plan."

"Why don't I have Kennedy schedule some time with you here at the spa, as well. That way you two can work on your magic while you get to know each other?"

"I would love that." Trin beamed. "May I ask you another question?"

"Of course."

"Do you ever think about Mama?"

Tears came quickly to Caris's eyes. "Yes. All the time."

IPSWICH, MASSACHUSETTS
1686

Kara heard her mama give Karina instructions to watch after them while she was gone, then promised a surprise if she and her sister behaved.

She and Kenna started sweeping and scrubbing the kitchen, hoping not to disappoint.

Once the cleaning was done, it was time to practice their magic—Kara's favorite part of the day.

Kenna suggested creating a spell to rid the house of dust,

but Karina quickly put her in her place and set them both to the task of working to master their water magic.

While Karina worked alone on her healing, Kara and Kenna pulled out the scrying bowl and filled it with water.

Kenna whispered, "I bet we look silly just staring at this bowl."

Kara giggled. "Perhaps, but if we develop our sight within its waves, who will look silly then?"

Kenna smiled and scrunched her brow, concentrating intently as she peered into the bowl.

Kara took a deep breath to clear her mind, opened her third eye, and cast her sight beyond the surface.

The waves began to ripple, and Kara closed her eyes. The blue of the sky filled her vision, a lovely image, until she realized it was being seen through her mother's eyes who lay hurt in a field.

Both girls gasped.

"What is it? Karina asked.

"Mama. There's something wrong with Mama," Kara exclaimed as Kenna started to cry.

"That was the worst day of my life," Caris sobbed. "I thought

I'd be forced to witness my own mother's death."

Trin leapt from the table and wrapped her arms around her sister. "I'm so sorry," Trin replied.

Caris pulled back and held Trin's gaze. "But it was also that day that I learned how strong and caring you were. I knew that once Mama left us, we would still be okay. Even until the very end, you refused to let anyone harm us. You are an amazing sister."

Trin's breath hitched. "Thank you, but look where it got us. Aren't you even the slightest bit mad at me for ruining our lives? I cast us and all of our kind to the wind. Sometimes I wonder if that was a selfish decision."

"If you had died that day, we'd have been left behind to suffer the same fate. I saw it and so did Kenna. You saved us all."

Trin closed her eyes and shook her head. "I'm so glad to have finally found you."

The buzzer beeped and Caris and Trin finalized their plans to meet later in the week to discuss what Jason had found. Hopefully it would be good news.

"Shadows lurk within and without, lies are afoot and

searching's about. Continue to twist and break their minds, for all will be mine in a matter of time." Once again he slit his wrist, dripping blood into the cauldron. "I will not falter, I will not fail, bless this charm by the crimson veil," he chanted the familiar words. Desperate times called for desperate measures. He leered at the jar sitting on his altar. The witch in Ipswich had a loose tongue, but he'd dealt with that. He roared with maniacal laughter as the blackened organ twitched within the glass.

Chapter Twenty-Seven

"It took me a couple days to schedule the dogs, and they're good, but not much use against magic," Jason explained. "I think the three of us should go back out together and try to find the trail ourselves."

"I'm up for that," Caris offered.

"Okay. Me too. When do you want to go? I have an appointment with Trin tomorrow, so maybe when I get home after that?" Kennedy suggested.

"Yeah. That sounds good. Let her know what we're up to and then hopefully by the next time either of you see her, we'll have something to share," Jason stated.

The siblings broke, moving to separate areas of the house

as they each prepared for the next day in their mundane lives.

"Do you have to be back in Washington anytime soon?" Jason asked Kennedy as he packed his lunch.

"No. My position with the FBI is extremely flexible," Kennedy winked and touched a finger to her temple. "Especially when I still have *some* magical abilities at my disposal."

Jason smirked. "Well, I'm sure glad you're on our side."

"Me too," Caris piped in. "But that begs the question. Why can't you just use the skill on Kit and force her to reveal where the cave is?"

Kennedy shrugged. "I may be able to manipulate human minds, but a demon's? I'm not sure I would have the same affect, and it's not a risk we can take without exposing what we know."

"True, true. All right, I guess that means we'll be needing our hiking gear," Caris replied.

"That, and some ingredients for the spell we'll most likely have to cast." Jason added.

"Okay, why don't you get the hiking stuff while I gather the supplies," Caris suggested.

"Why? What's wrong cuz, don't want to go digging around that dirty garage of ours?" Jason teased, knowing his cousin hated that cobweb infested outbuilding.

"You got that right!"

"I'll go with," Kennedy offered, joining Jason as he headed out the back door.

"You're a couple of brave souls, the both of ya!" Caris called.

Caris moved to the breakfast nook and began assembling her ingredients at the makeshift workspace they'd set up. She'd chosen lemon grass to provide clarity of mind in addition to its bonus ability of repelling snakes, grabbed some sulfur to ward off any demonic presence, and tossed in some angelica root for protection and to boost her and Kennedy's female power. Caris gathered salt, candles and rope, and lastly the box containing the demon's tooth before she took a seat. She'd completed the ritual of filling her basket, just as she'd done so many centuries ago.

IPSWICH, MASSACHUESETTS
1690

"Kara, have you packed everything we'll need?" Karina asked.

"Yes, sister. It's all prepared. Thank you for letting me come to the celebration this year. It's my first official Beltane as a matured woman." Kara spun around. "Do you think I'll find my soul mate at the bonfire, or perhaps at the maypole dance?" Kara beamed.

"Perhaps, sister. Anything is possible when the God and Goddess join under the stars."

"Do you want to see the wreath I made for my hair? I can make you one too, if you'd like." Kara excitedly pulled the flower ring from her basket, displaying roses, daisies, and sprigs of baby's breath.

"It's lovely, Kara. But we need to be on our way, so gather your cloak and let's prepare to depart."

Kara watched her older sister as she tasked Kenna with specific chores while they were gone. Kenna, of course, was not pleased she'd be left behind, but with her healing touch, Karina smoothed her dismay and set extra protections in place as she kissed her farewell.

Karina and Kara left Kenna and the hound safely in place and ventured onto the path that would lead to the Epps estate on Castle Hill. Daniel Epps was too old for Kara, but his son, Lionel, had taken a shine to her when they last met in town. Kara smiled at the potential union the magic of this night may bring.

"Caris. What in the world? You're flush and have a lovelorn look about you?" Kennedy said as she fanned her face.

"Oh my, I'm so sorry. I was lost in a memory."

"Looks like a fine memory to me," Jason teased.

Caris jumped from her chair and smoothed her t-shirt. "Let's just say, I'll be damn happy when all this is over and we can *all* move on with our lives. We've sacrificed enough."

Caris felt two sets of arms encircle her and could no longer hold back her emotions. Tears streaked her cheeks for the lost potential her previous lives had held. So many lost loved ones, missed opportunities to have children, passing of the ones she tried to start a family with, and every single time, their destiny had gotten in the way.

"You're right, Car. It's time we put a stop to this, and with Trin's help, you can be damn sure we're gonna kick some ass," Kennedy stated, boosting their spirits.

Chapter Twenty-Eight

Trin closed her eyes and concentrated on the feel of Kennedy's hand in hers. The witches ladder wrapped around both their wrists, snaking up their arms as they increased the amount of power between them. Blue sparks flared when they reached the peak of their meditation.

"Dang it." Trin sighed. "I can feel our bond strong and true, but it lies just beneath the fog of Kit's barrier."

Kennedy smiled. "We'll break through soon, I'm sure of it. Besides, if we're successful tonight, this could all be over."

"Very true. But promise me you'll all be careful." Trin hugged her little sister and waved goodbye as she left the massage room.

They'd spent the first part of their hour-and-a-half together simply talking and reminiscing. It hadn't taken long for the two of them to become reacquainted, and Trin's pride at how strong and capable her little sister turned out to be grew exponentially. They had a few more visits lined up, as Trin had made sure she was booked solid this week. The less time she spent at home, the better. Kit hadn't pushed her any further about her impromptu getaway or the Hardy's intrusion into their lives, which was great. But it also felt as though Kit was just biding her time.

"Have a great night, Mia. I'll see you tomorrow." Trin waved to the receptionist and pushed out the door.

The setting sun cast the perfect hue against the evening sky. Dusk was Trin's favorite time of day, except for lately when it meant she'd have to face her "*sister.*" Trin climbed into her car and took a moment to reinforce her mental blocks before turning the key. She had to stay strong so that Caris, Jason, and Kennedy could move forward with their plan tonight.

She'd devised multiple scenarios as to how she could join them tonight for their trip to the woods, but in the end, she knew it wasn't possible since she was meant to serve as the distraction.

Kennedy had expressed concern that Kit might be able to sense someone nearing her power source, so Jason had suggested a sister's night out, hoping dinner and a movie would keep Kit occupied for at least a few hours during their search.

Trin reached for her cell phone and typed out a message.

Trin: *All done. See you at Milano's in a few.*

Kit: *Sounds great. I'll be there.*

Trin took every side street she could, creeping at a snail's pace while heading towards the restaurant. Kit had suggested the pizza place closer to the spa, but since she needed to waste as much time as possible, Trin opted for Italian food, knowing it would take at least an hour to get through dinner.

"Hey," Trin greeted Kit as she slid into the booth.

"Hi. How was your day?" Kit asked with a smile on her face.

"It was good. Busy."

The waitress arrived with their menus within a split second of Trin taking a seat. *Dammit, slow down*, Trin thought. Why the one time she needed to *waste* time, everyone was the picture of proficiency?

"Thanks," Kit offered, placing her order without even looking at the menu. "I'll have the chicken parmesan with a Caesar salad, dressing on the side, please."

Kit looked up and smiled, causing Trin to have a severe deer-in-the-headlights moment.

"Um...actually, can I have a few minutes?" Trin asked the waitress.

"Of course. Can I get you both started with something to drink?"

"I'll have a water," Kit answered.

Trin swallowed hard. "I'll take a glass of your pinot noir, please."

"Pinot noir? That's not your usual poison," Kit teased.

"Yeah, I think I'm going to try some new things tonight." Trin forced a smile that she was sure didn't reach her eyes. Hearing Kit throw around words like *poison* had a different effect on her now, making it clear that this was going to be more difficult than Trin thought.

Trin buried her head in the menu, trying to think of something to eat that wasn't her usual fare, but would still be good and hopefully take a long time to prepare. She ordered as soon as the waitress returned with their drinks. "I'll start with an order of risotto, then have the pork lasagna and a side salad. Oil and vinegar on the side please." Trin handed back the menu and looked up to find Kit staring at her with opened-mouth suspicion.

"What?"

Kit shook her head, "I've never seen you order that much food. Are you feeling okay?"

Trin faked a laugh. "I told you I wanted to try new things, and after the busy schedule I've had lately, I'm running low on energy." Trin patted her stomach. "Bring on the food."

Kit cocked a brow. "And about ten extra pounds."

"Well, it's not like I'm seeing anyone, so that shouldn't matter." Trin couldn't help herself. She knew her snide comment would bring Jason's name into the mix, but maybe if they talked about her lost chance at love, that would help prove to Kit that she'd truly cast him aside.

"Just because you've been deceived by a local Wiccan hottie, doesn't mean you won't find someone else," Kit snapped.

Trin's nostrils flared as she clenched her jaw. She took a deep breath and reinforced her mental blocks. "You're right, I guess, and honestly, I'm not looking to start a relationship with anyone right now. I'm not ready. Besides, it's not like I want kids anytime soon." Trin shrugged and prayed her lie was convincing.

Kit's head jerked to the crying baby across the restaurant and Trin witnessed something she'd never seen before. Pure anger radiated from Kit's entire body. If Trin opened her third eye right now, she had no doubt she'd see a bright red haze surrounding their table.

"Kit. What's wrong?" Trin asked, nervous to know the real answer.

"Nothing." Kit shook her head, visibly forcing herself to relax. "I just don't understand why parents bring infant children to public places. It's like they have no respect for others."

Trin frowned and took a sip of her wine, trying to process the odd comment. Thinking back, though, she couldn't remember a time in this life or the past where Kit had shown any interest in children. *Weird.*

Trin spent the rest of the meal trying to lighten the mood and searched for anything that would keep Kit engaged. Wiping the corners of her mouth she leaned back in the booth and checked her watch. "So, what movie do you want to see?"

"Are you still able to move with all that food in you?" Kit joked.

Stuffed to the gills, Trin stretched, miserable inside but convincing none the less. "You betcha."

Kit chuckled and slid out of her seat. "Maybe we should go dancing instead. Burn some of this off."

"Nope. I'll exercise tomorrow. Tonight, we're relaxing." Trin waddled all the way to her car.

"Do you want to drive separate or just ride with me?" Kit asked.

Knowing she'd need to check in with the Hardys', Trin quickly opted for the first. "I'll drive. I don't want to have to come back for my car later."

"Okay. Meet you there."

Kit was the first to leave the parking lot, giving Trin the moment she needed to send a message.

Trin: *Leaving the restaurant. Heading to the movie. You've got 2 hours.*

Jason: *Thanks. About to cast spell. Be careful.*

Trin: *You too.*

Trin erased the messages and put her car in drive, making a beeline for the theatre. They'd be watching some Jane Austen-ish romance Kit had suggested, which was fine by her, since the play time was one hour and fifty-eight minutes.

Pulling into a parking space at the far end of the lot, Trin searched for Kit's car, which was nowhere to be seen.

Recalling Jason's last words, Trin cussed. "Oh shit!"

Chapter Twenty-Nine

"Do we have everything?" Jason asked.

"Yep. All the hiking stuff is loaded, and Caris already climbed into the back seat with her basket." Kennedy winked.

"Okay. Let's do this." Jason jumped into the driver's seat of Caris's Jeep. He'd bookmarked the location of where he'd been left on his GPS and was anxious to reach the spot as soon as possible.

Trin was going to be keeping Kit busy tonight with a dinner and a movie, which meant they'd only have around four hours, including travel time.

"Do you have the tooth?" Jason asked.

"Yes. I have everything we need," Caris reassured.

In Jason's mind, it was no coincidence tonight was the new moon. The timing of everything seemed to be on their side, which left him excited and confident about their plan.

"Let's cast a cloaking spell from inside the Jeep when we get close. That way, we can block our presence from the get go," Jason suggested.

"Good idea. Just let me know when to start," Caris replied.

They drove in silence for forty minutes until Jason gave the signal.

Kennedy turned around at Caris's instruction and watched as her sister sprinkled angelica root into the palm of her hand. Reaching for hers, Caris began to chant once their fingers were entwined. "Goddess dark, like the moon, we ask you shield us from evil's view. Boost our strength and hide our link, as we search for the source we seek. So mote it be."

"So mote it be," Kennedy and Jason intoned.

A silver energy burst from the girls' hands, settling over the entire Jeep like a protective, transparent bubble.

"Great job, Car." Kennedy smiled and turned around just as they rolled to a stop.

"We're here," Jason announced.

With the Jeep safely off the road, they all climbed out and retrieved their gear. "I figure a straight cut through here would be our best bet to start. Then, once we reach this clearing we'll cast the spell." Jason folded his map and took the basket from

Caris who fell in line between him and Kennedy.

They hiked in silence and on full alert. After thirty-five minutes, night had fallen. They paused for a drink and to retrieve their flashlights at Caris's suggestion. She thought it best if they didn't use magic until absolutely necessary. So, after checking the compass, Jason led on, following the small beam of light.

The hike was easy, the terrain mostly flat and compact, but the lack of light was definitely becoming a hindrance.

"Car, do you think we could do something to boost the flashlights' output? That way we're not casting a spell for light, but simply enhancing the mechanism?" Kennedy asked.

"Sure. We can try."

Jason sat the basket on the ground and took a seat on a fallen tree trunk while the girls worked.

"Here, take this." Caris handed Jason the end of a red rope. "Wrap it around your flashlight then your wrist."

Jason stood and did as he was told, then waited as Caris took the middle of the rope and repeated the process herself, then had Kennedy do the same with the end. With their hands bound in a tight circle, the light cast from their flashlights shot straight up into the night sky.

"Charge this light, brightest bright, concealed within our space this night. Never to be seen but by us three, as I will it so mote it be."

Kennedy laughed out loud when they were suddenly bathed in a bright white light that filled up their protective bubble. It looked like they were encased in a miniature version of the sun.

"Damn, Caris. I didn't realize you were getting so good," Jason boasted.

"I think working with Trin and Kennedy has definitely boosted my powers. They're not fully restored, but we're definitely on the right path."

"Well, I hope that's not the only path we're on that's right. We need to hurry this along if we're going to get out of here before Trin's ruse is up," Kennedy piped in.

"You're right. Let's get going." Jason untied them all from the rope, stuffing it in his pocket, then took off again at a clipped pace.

In just under an hour later, they'd reached the clearing.

"The hills begin to rise from here, so I think the chance of us finding a cave in the area is pretty high," Jason expressed, placing the basket in the center of the small meadow. He and Kennedy patrolled the boundary while Caris set up her tools. About halfway through his scan of the woods, his phone buzzed. It was Trin.

Trin: *Leaving the restaurant. Heading to the movie. You've got 2 hours.*

Jason quickly typed out his reply.

Jason: *Thanks. About to cast spell. Be careful.*

Trin: *You too.*

"Okay, come on," Caris announced minutes later, her timing spot on.

Gathering around the makeshift altar, Caris handed each of them a candle to hold, then cast her circle using the salt she'd packed. "I cast this circle, once around, all within magic bound. Earth and dust, salt and sea, protected now, by one by three."

Caris nodded at Kennedy, who flicked a finger and set their candles alight, and then began her chant. "Fire strong, fire bright, guide our passion on this night. Reveal what's hidden that we seek, evil's lair, curses keep."

They each smiled as the flame on all three candles elongated and pulled in one common direction.

Caris moved to the altar and placed the lemongrass and sulfur in her pestle and mortar, then gently retrieved the black box that contained the demon's tooth.

Sliding off the lid, Caris carefully pulled back the black satin cloth and used its corner to grab and toss the shard into the mix.

The sulfur bubbled around the tooth, dampening its vibration. Taking a deep breath, Caris opened her mind and inhaled the smoke.

Transported instantly, Caris flew through the night sky,

joined by Kennedy and Jason's astral bodies on the hunt. Jason's thoughts pricked her mind as he plotted the land that passed below. Kennedy used her mental clarity to search the woods for any sentient presence, while Caris opened her heart in an effort to sense any magic in the air.

Hills rolled and grew in size, merging with rocky buttes and small creeks. Waterfalls ran nearby as they continued to soar deep within an untouched part of the forest. Jason finally pointed to what looked like a small crack within the rock face. As they touched down, Kennedy put up a hand, stilling their movements. She used her mental link to share her thoughts. *"There is definitely something evil residing within this cave."*

"I agree. I can see a red aura radiating from within," Caris added.

"This is it. I've marked the location. Now, let's get back to our bodies and return for real," Jason stated.

With the speed of the Goddess they were all hurtled back into their physical bodies, aware and ready to face what was coming next.

Caris closed the circle, carefully depositing the demon's tooth back into the box and placing it in her pocket. Jason quickly gathered their flashlights and checked his map, preparing to retrace the trek back towards the cave.

Kennedy grabbed her service pistol from her bag and shrugged when Caris cast her a skeptical glance. "What? We have no idea what's going to be in there. Besides, it makes me feel better."

Jason laughed and could obviously relate. He too had brought his gun and winked at Caris as he withdrew it from his back holster. "It should only take about twenty-five minutes to get there on foot, so we should have plenty of time to search the cave and destroy his power at its source."

Kennedy and Caris nodded and fell in step. An anxious excitement could be felt in the air, and with any luck, this curse would be over in a few minutes and their powers fully restored.

Jason brought them to a halt outside the mouth of the cave. He crouched down in the bushes next to the opening and whispered to the girls. "Caris, do we just go in, or should we cast a spell from here?"

"We already have our protection in place, so let's go in and have a look around. Kennedy, be on the lookout for an old talisman, something that's tying him to this place."

Kennedy and Jason both nodded and gripped their guns a little tighter as they all crept forward.

Suddenly, a massive blast of air threw them backwards onto the ground. A loud screech resonated from inside the cave followed by a thick black fog that billowed from the opening.

Caris screamed and Kennedy gasped as they all squirmed to get away from the demon's face that had taken shape within the fog.

"He's in there, Jason. We have to get out of here." Caris

grabbed her pocket, trying like hell to keep the box from ripping its way out of her jeans.

Jason gathered the girls and ran back the way they came as an eerie laughter echoed off the hills.

Chapter Thirty

"Trin. What the hell happened?" Jason's message confirmed her fears.

Trin had arrived home to an empty house and thought the worse. At least hearing Jason's voice meant he was okay. She quickly dialed his number.

"Jason. Is everyone okay? Did she hurt you?"

All Trin wanted to do was race straight to the Hardy's and wrap herself in Jason's arms, but that was still not an option. They had to maintain the distance they'd been keeping, in case this ruse was something that needed to continue.

"Trin. We're all fine, but Kit was there. She cast a banishment from inside the cave that knocked us all on our asses."

"I don't understand how she could have gotten there that fast. She was literally out of my sight for no more than five minutes while we drove to the theatre."

"Well, you of all people should know how powerful magic can be. I'm sure she just teleported into the cave when she sensed someone was near."

"That or she has it booby-trapped," Kennedy called out.

"At least you found it. When do you think we can all go back together and end this?" Trin asked.

"Caris isn't sure. She thinks we missed an opportunity tonight by not having you with us on the new moon. She's going to do some scrying and try to pinpoint the best time for us to try again."

"Okay, but what the hell am I supposed to do until then? Kit probably knows I was involved."

"Involved with what?" Kit's voice sounded from behind her.

"Hey!" Trin spun around, wide-eyed and petrified. She debated hanging up, but knowing Jason was still listening on the other end of their call gave her a small measure of comfort.

"Sorry I had to bail. I got a call from Harold who demanded I meet him immediately to discuss tomorrow night's celebration, which from the sound of it, you already know about. Are you in on this damn party, too?" Kit smiled as she set her purse on the table.

An excruciating laugh tore from Trin's throat. "Dang it! It was supposed to be a surprise."

"Well, you guys blew it then, because the second Harold said he was in town, I knew something was up. He hates traveling this far North." Kit laughed and waved goodnight as she climbed the stairs.

Trin waiting for Kit's bedroom door to close then whispered, "Did you hear all that?"

"Yes. It sounds like Kennedy was right, the place was booby-trapped, and it looks like you have a party to go to tomorrow night," Jason replied.

"Oh joy!"

"Bone and blood, spirit and soul, ripped from them, my only goal. Set a trap, fall in line, all their magic will soon be mine." The potion boiled and churned, sending up a gray mist that turned into a protective net, taking on the shape of a massive tangle of spider webs. He smiled as they attached themselves to the walls and ceiling. He was ready...all he needed now was the bait.

"What time should I be at the restaurant?" Trin asked between sips of her coffee.

"Harold says we're to meet him at 7:00pm. Will that give you enough time to get home from work and change?" Kit questioned.

"Yep. I'll be there with bells on." Trin swallowed the bitter taste the words left in her mouth. Suppressing her anger was becoming more and more difficult, since every time she looked at Kit, all she saw was centuries of betrayal. There had been numerous times over the past week where Trin wanted to scream from the top of her lungs, *"I know who you are and what you've done."* But after what happened last night, and the fact that they were so close to putting an end to this charade, she forced herself to remain diligent and stay on task. Willpower was a weapon she'd continue to hone.

"Great. I'll see you there." Kit was dressed in her usual painting gear: a t-shirt, baggy overalls, and bare feet, which meant she'd be spending the day upstairs in the room they'd set up as her studio.

Trin finished her coffee and left for the spa, anxious for her mid-day appointment with Caris. Jason had reassured her that everything was fine, but she wanted to hear Caris's side of the story as well. She needed to see if there were any details that she could pick out that maybe they had missed.

"Good morning, Mia." Trin offered her usual greeting to the receptionist and proceeded straight to the locker room to start her day.

Five hours later and it was finally time for Caris's appointment.

"Okay, so tell me everything." Trin hopped onto the table, happy to be off her feet.

"Well, Jason pretty much summed it up. We came to the clearing and cast our searching spell which worked great. We all flew through the astral plane and located the source with no problem. Then, once we were physically there and about to go in, a blast of air and fog burst from the mouth of the cave. There was this creepy demon's face inside of it," Caris shuttered.

"It makes me sick to know that that is Kit. I still can't wrap my head around it."

Caris took Trin's hand in hers. "I know it must be hard, but Trin, you're going to have to come to terms with this, because soon...we're going to need to do whatever is necessary to put an end to this."

"I know," Trin sighed. "I'll be ready."

Caris smiled and handed Trin a pouch of angelica root. "Here. Keep this in your pocket. I'm sure you're aware that it's great for protection and boosts female power, and this is some of the stuff Kennedy and I used the other night. It should help strengthen our connection."

"Great! Thanks!" Trin tucked the white cotton satchel into her pocket and instantly felt at peace. "Have you worked out when we should go back to the cave?"

"No. Not yet. The full moon is only a week away now, but it still doesn't seem to be lining up with the spell."

"Is there anything I can do to help from here," Trin motioned around the private room.

Caris cocked her head. "Maybe. Let me do some more work tonight. Kennedy and I will both book appointments before the full moon and I'll fill you in then."

Trin smiled and hugged her sister, anxious to finally be able to contribute in at least some small way. Following Caris out to the front room, she waved goodbye before pulling her next chart.

"Trin?"

Trin spun around at the sound of Kit's voice. "What are you doing here?" Trin asked nervously.

"Harold called and bumped up the time of the party. I brought you your dress so you wouldn't be late." Kit glared out the window as Caris pulled away in her Jeep. "Isn't that your teacher friend?" Kit leaned in. "I thought you were staying away from them?" she whispered.

Trin took a step back and squared her shoulders. "I can't control who books appointments with me."

Trin swore she could see fire sparking behind Kit's eyes. "It may only be a massage to you, but if they are the ones causing the problems, then even the slightest touch could be fueling their means. You need to remove her from your approved client list, Trin. For your own good."

Kit pushed the garment bag into her hands and left without another word. Fuming, Trin raced into the locker room to dial Caris and quickly left a message when she didn't answer. "Kit was here and saw you leave. Please be careful and call me once you're safely home."

An energy ball flew from Trin's hand, denting the door of her locker. Trin collapsed onto a bench, forcing a few deep breaths in an effort to calm down. They needed to bring this to an end and soon, but first she had one more appointment to get through and a party to attend.

Trin walked to the sink and splashed some water on her face, and then returned to the front to greet her next client.

Just as she glanced at the file, the door to the waiting room swung open. "My turn," said the very sexy Mr. Hardy.

Chapter Thirty-One

"Oh my god, what are you doing? Kit was just here, did she see you?" Trin pulled Jason down the hall and into her assigned room.

"Calm down. No, she didn't see me."

Trin tossed his chart onto the counter. "I can't believe you. Why didn't Caris tell me you were coming?"

"Because she didn't know. Christ, I didn't know I'd be scheduling a massage just so I could see my girlfriend, but dammit Trin, I miss you."

"I miss you, too, but we can't risk anything right now, Jason," she snapped as she leaned back against the door.

"I get that you're worried, but if all I can get is a few stolen moments with you, I'm going to take them, risk or no risk."

Trin crossed her arms in front of her chest trying to tamp down her anger. Between pretending with Kit, worrying over her sisters, and now coming face-to-face with the fact that she had a man in her life to adjust to, it was all leaving her extremely pent up.

Jason smirked at Trin.

"What's so funny? This whole situation is screwed up," Trin said as she smacked his arm, sending a blue shock arcing between them.

"It's been a long time since I've seen the feisty side of you."

She narrowed her eyes at him.

"Don't you remember how we defused our frustrations back in the day?"

She bit her bottom lip as memories flooded her mind.

Jason unclasped her arms and raised them above her head, rubbing the vein at her wrist as he slowly and deliberately kissed her neck, the tension in her body releasing with each stroke of his thumb.

The caress of his lips and the kneading of his skillful hands had Trin casting a silencing spell over the room. Never before had she been naked at her place of business, but today, her emotions had been pushed to their limit and she'd be breaking all the rules.

Trin stripped, unabashed as Jason did the same. She guided him to lie back on the table and proceeded to climb atop him with a wicked smile.

"This isn't how I imagined our first time in this life," Jason panted as Trin kissed along his neck, "but our souls are connected just as they were centuries ago, and I crave you now as much as I did then."

"I feel it too."

Trin crushed her lips to his as she lowered herself onto him. Their passion flared and in a rush the room began to spin. Their connection was more than physical, it was spiritual, magical, and Trin could feel the buzz of energy in the air.

Lost in each other, the memories of their time together floated between them as their minds began to link. A lifetime of love sent their spirits soaring as their ecstasy peaked. Trin opened herself in that moment, heart and soul, and knew in an instant what they needed to do.

Refreshed and dressed in her black corseted dress of tulle and satin, Trin waved to Mia, chuckling internally, as she left for the day. Her rendezvous with Jason may have been taboo, but it was worth the risk.

Trin drove straight to the party, hoping a brief appearance would be enough because there were preparations that needed to be made, and she couldn't wait to get to the Hardy's as soon as possible. There was no reason to hide anymore, for the answer came in not being apart, but finally coming together.

Trin took a deep breath and shored up her mental blocks before entering the restaurant. She may be ready to take down Kit, but there was no point in doing it here.

Kit greeted Trin with a hug and smile and began to introduce her to her inner circle. Trin had met Harold before, but these were not only people Kit worked with, but apparently, some of her clients and colleagues were in attendance as well. They were all here to acknowledge and award Kit's achievements within the art community, which Trin now questioned as authentic or not. Even with all the falseness surrounding Kit, Trin thought that when it came to her art, she was the real deal. But now, she questioned whether that was even true. It was impossible to tell when magic and lies were involved.

"Thank you for coming, Trin. It means so much to have you here," Kit whispered in her ear.

"You're welcome." Trin forced a smile.

Grabbing a glass of champagne, Trin retrieved her cell phone from her small silver clutch and frowned at the display. No call or text from Caris yet. Perhaps she'd had other errands to run before heading home? A slow chill rolled across Trin's skin.

"Everyone, gather around please," Harold announced from the front of the room. "Thank you all for joining us tonight to honor Kit Callaway. For anyone who has ever had the pleasure of viewing one of her pieces, I'm sure you'd all agree that her art comes straight from her heart and soul. Her classic lines and ethereal concepts spark imagination and will continue to span time, inspiring future generations to come." Harold raised his glass. "And she's made my company a lot of money, so cheers!" he joked.

"Cheers," the crowd responded.

Kit stepped up to the podium, red-cheeked in her white pantsuit. "Thanks, Harold. It's nice to know how you really feel." The crowd roared with laughter. "My inspiration comes from the world around me, and I'm so grateful I've been blessed with the talent to turn that into something you all can enjoy. It means a great deal to me that you'd accept me and what I do in a society that has such varied tastes. I've found my niche and I couldn't be more honored that you're all a part of it. Thank you for coming."

Trin raised her glass, conflicted by the emotions she was feeling. She hated Kit for deceiving her, for being the evil that had kept her from her true sisters for over three hundred years. But at the same time, those shared lifetimes weren't something one could easily forget. Trin would end Kit for what she'd done, but she was also genuinely proud of her accomplishments here tonight. It was confusing.

"Trin, are you okay?" Kit asked, pulling her from her thoughts.

"Yes, I'm okay. Your speech was nice. I'm happy for you, Kit."

"Thanks. Will you join me at the head table? Dinner is about to be served."

Trin clutched her purse, the phone inside burning a hole through her subconscious. "Actually, I'm going to head home. I'm not feeling all that well."

Kit frowned and grabbed Trin's arm. "Maybe a bite to eat would help. You haven't been taking very good care of yourself lately, sister."

"You're right. I've been feeling pretty drained lately, so like I said, I think I'll be heading home." Trin yanked her arm from Kit's grasp. "Enjoy your party."

Trin's stomach was in knots as she stomped out of the restaurant. Of course Kit knew she was feeling drained, it was her damn fault!

Trin drove straight to the Hardy's and couldn't care less if Kit knew it or not.

"Trin! What the hell are you doing here? You're supposed to stay away until Caris nails down the proper time for our next spell," Kennedy exclaimed.

"There's no time for that. I think she has Caris," Trin rushed to explain.

"What?" Jason rounded the corner of the kitchen.

"Kit saw her with me today at the spa, and I haven't heard from her since."

"Dammit!" Kennedy cursed, collapsing onto the couch. She punched Caris's number into her phone but received no answer.

"Trin. You should go back to the party and keep Kit occupied and we'll head to the cave," Jason instructed.

"No! That's just it." Trin reached for his hand, igniting a blue spark between them. "Tonight, when we consummated our relationship anew, I saw what we needed to do."

Kennedy snapped her head in Trin's direction. "Do tell, sister."

"The fact that we've been staying apart has been our mistake and exactly what Kit has wanted all along. It's when we truly come back together that we'll be a threat. A threat to breaking through whatever block she has us on. We need to return to the cave to get Caris *together*. All of us."

"I don't understand. We've all been together before and couldn't break through the block? What's different now?" Kennedy asked.

"I'm different. The physical connection of being intimate with Jason unlocked something within me. I saw clearly what we need to do."

"What if Caris isn't at the cave. What if Kit took her somewhere else since she knows we found her lair?" Jason interjected.

"No. She'll still take her there. You said it yourself, that place is connected to the source of her power."

"It makes me crazy to address her in the feminine when we all know what *she* really is," Jason spat.

"He...she...what does it matter? As soon as we find Caris this will all be over," Trin said with a firm set to her jaw. "The moon may not be full yet, but together, I know we can save Caris and put a stop to this," Trin proclaimed. "Besides, I'm sick of waiting for her to make a move. Now, if you'd be so kind, can you show me to your supplies?"

Chapter Thirty-Two

Kennedy led the way, showing Trin to their temporary work area and helped gather the items.

"Salt, sulfur, and houndstooth," Trin instructed.

Kennedy placed the items in the basket and stifled a sob at the thought of Caris.

Trin placed a hand on the basket, understanding the connection. "Breaking through Kit's block is obviously going to take more than just the three of us being in the same room." Trin glanced at Jason. "So, while I set up the spell, you two will have to keep her distracted. Keep her talking and focused on your attempts to save Caris."

"Okay. Monologuing. Got it." Kennedy smiled.

Trin laughed and turned. "I've got everything I need from here, but I have to stop by my house on our way out of town."

"Do you really think that's a good idea?" Jason asked.

"Kit won't be there. If she's not still at her party then she'll be in the cave," Trin assured him.

"Okay, then. It looks like we're ready to go." Jason's less than enthusiastic demeanor had Trin hanging back.

"Hey? Are you okay?" she asked.

Jason planted his feet and crossed his arms. "I'm worried we're rushing into this. The idea of any of you being put in danger, just because we're all mad and impatient has me concerned," Jason confessed.

"As always, my caring companion." Trin stared at Jason, seeing Jeremiah's spirit within. "I know that's how it seems, but trust me, I know what I'm doing."

"The last time you said that, you ended up on the pyre," Jason stated.

Trin placed her hands on his arms, pushing them open so she could step into his embrace. "Our physical connection unlocked the answer for me, and you know better than anyone what I would do to save my sisters. I wouldn't risk them if I thought we would fail."

Jason leaned down and placed a kiss on her lips. "Yes. You're right. I know you wouldn't."

Trin and Jason walked hand in hand to his truck. Climbing

in, they headed straight to Trin's house.

"What am I looking for?" Jason asked, since he refused to let her go inside.

"A red box sitting on my dresser. You can't miss it." Trin smiled.

Jason took Trin's keys and quickly made his way inside. The house was empty, just as Trin had foretold.

Jason raced upstairs, finding the box exactly where Trin said it would be and immediately returned to the truck. Settled back behind the wheel, he handed the small box across to Trin. "Here you go."

"Thank you. We're all set."

"Are you sure you have everything we'll need?" Kennedy asked from the backseat.

"I have enough, but it's not the supplies that will beat Kit, it's us...together."

"That sounds vague and completely irrational. We're going to be facing a centuries old demon whose soul has been fused to yours, and you're basically saying we should just wing it?" Kennedy shook her head with a quirky grin on her face.

"What I'm saying is you should trust me," Trin took her sister's hand and opened her heart and mind. Memories of the three of them together and the magic they used to openly work filled her thoughts. She could sense young Kenna awakening within Kennedy, stirring and ready to join the fight.

Kennedy removed her hand and stared up at her sister. "It's you, Karina. I felt you."

"That's what I'm saying. A portion of me has been released, and it's the blood bond we share as sisters that will break through Kit's blocks. And whether she knows it or not, once we all connect, there'll be nothing she can do to stop us."

Kennedy smiled from ear to ear, then looked at Jason through the rearview mirror. "Step on it, cousin. We've got a demon to destroy."

Caris worked the ropes behind her back until her wrists were raw.

"You won't escape, child, so you might want to save your strength."

"Fuck you! We know who you are...*Kit*, and I know you can feel them coming," Caris taunted.

A hoarse laughter, like glass on sandpaper, echoed off the cave walls. "You know nothing."

Caris swallowed past the lump in her throat as she watched the cloaked demon stir his cauldron. A foul green fog slithered from the bowl and coated the floor, rising up to fill the opening of the cave. Solidifying and turning invisible, it sealed the door to her escape or rescue. Tears built behind Caris's eyes as she thought of what would happen if her family ran into the barrier.

"Please, just let me go."

"It's too late for that," he hissed, tying a gag around her mouth. "You're right. They are coming, and soon, you will all be mine."

Jason pulled off the road in the same spot as before. "Okay, it's about a two-hour hike to the cave from here."

"We don't have time for that," Trin snapped. "Give me your hands."

"What should I do with this?" Kennedy pointed to the basket.

"Put the sachets in your pockets," Trin replied.

Kennedy emptied the contents into her pants then exited the truck. Gathered in a circle, the three of them joined hands.

"Goddess of the moon, stars, and sun, transport us so that this may be done. Ending the evil, righting a wrong, guided by your loving tongue. Let your words flow through me, as I will it, so mote it be." The air spun and lightning flashed as Trin was filled with the moon mother's magic.

The girl's auburn hair soared upward into a vortex as they were transported to their destination, their feet touching down just outside the cave. Jason shook his head and winked at Trin, giving his silent appreciation of her exceedingly impressive new skills.

Trin cast her thoughts into their minds, *"Give me a moment to scan the cave and then...follow my lead."*

Weary, Kennedy took a deep breath but stood resolute. Jason pulled a talisman from his pocket and slipped it around his neck. Trin beamed. It was a worn leather cord, bearing the ring Jeremiah presented to Karina all those years ago. *"I thought this might help our connection,"* he thought.

Trin caressed his cheek and placed a kiss upon his lips. *"Our connection has never been stronger. I love you."*

"And I you."

Jason and Kennedy stepped behind Trin as she moved towards the opening of the cave. Using the motion of her hands to gather energy, Trin cast runes by drawing specific glyphs in the air. A blue energy circled before her, pulsing with magic and a piercing focus. She slashed her hand towards the cave and watched as her spell ate up the green barrier blocking their way.

Trin stepped forward, motioning for Jason and Kennedy to follow. Twenty steps in, they rounded the bend and entered the heart of the cave. Caris sat tied against the wall, alive and seemingly unharmed.

Kennedy raced to untie her sister while Jason stood guard, allowing Trin to start setting up the spell in her mind.

"It's a trap!" Caris cried as soon as her gag was removed.

"Of course it is," Trin calmly replied. *"Join hands with Kennedy, and slowly move towards me,"* Trin sent into Caris's mind, surprising her by the sudden connection.

The girls did as instructed, forming a wall with Jason in front of Trin, as she faced the demon's altar.

"Come out and face us, foul beast. It's time you stopped your lies and deceit," Kennedy commanded.

A thick black fog rolled across the floor accompanied by a sinister laugh and two beady-red eyes emerging from the shadows.

"You haven't seemed to mind the years we've spent together. Always happy and well protected. It's only now that your life is in real danger. I told you, you should have stayed away from them." Kit's voice sounded from behind them all.

They all spun around, confused, and saw Kit standing there in her white-pant suit, while the cloaked demon continued to drift at them from the other side of the room.

"What the hell is this?" Jason yelled.

"Stop with the theatrics, Kit. I know it's you. Drop whatever illusion this is and show your true form, *Heinrich,*" Trin commanded.

"How dare you speak his name!" Kit bellowed, launching herself at Trin.

Kennedy pushed past her sister and in a swift move, blew a cloud of houndstooth into Kit's face, immobilizing her where she stood. "Be still like the dog you are," Kennedy spat.

With a quick glance behind them, Trin summoned the witches ladder from her purse and linked hands with her sisters. "Show yourself to the three, demon of old shall it be, strip away the false and fake, only truth will the Goddess take."

Trin opened her eyes and gasped. The demon remained the same, cloaked and glowering from the shadows, while Kit stood transformed, wearing a pilgrim dress and holding a phantom child.

"Ann Putnam?" Trin gasped.

"That's right, *sister*. Did you think you were the only witch who was tied to the devil?"

The demon cackled and lunged towards his altar but met an invisible barrier when Trin threw up her hand.

"Explain! Now!" Trin demanded.

"What's there to say? Heinrich found me long ago, long before you, and in order to spare my life, I made a bargain."

"What kind of bargain?" Caris spat.

"To hunt witches by pretending to be mortal and in need." She jostled the small apparition in her arms. "How was I to know that Karina's spell would pull us all through time, forever linked and dependent upon her energy alone to survive?"

The demon began chanting while it writhed against Trin's shield. Luckily, just as she'd foreseen, the magic between her and her sisters was silently building below the surface. Trin could feel Karina, Caris, Kara, Kennedy, and Kenna, as if each of their signatures was unique and powerful in and of itself. She had to keep talking while the Goddess's magic unfused the red connection that was twisted between her, Ann, and the demon.

"So, all this time it was you who found me and invaded my life, not Heinrich?" Trin asked, genuinely curious.

"In a matter of speaking. Heinrich and I are linked, as I am to you, but he's bound to this cave and depends on me to keep him well fed." She raised her chin.

"You mean by bringing him blood and magic? Witches to the slaughter," Kennedy spat, appalled.

"That's right. As long as I kept the three of you apart and played my role, my bargain remained intact."

Kennedy looked between her sisters and smiled wide. "Guess you're shit out of luck then."

Ann's eyes fluttered between the girls and the demon. Her failure was clear and so was her panic. She never questioned why she needed to keep the three apart, but now, as the binds that had connected them for so long were being stripped away, she realized she was doomed. Unlinked, she was just another witch for Heinrich to feed upon.

The demon clapped his hands and a resonating boom echoed from the walls, causing Trin's shield to shake and weaken. Ann floated through the air towards Heinrich's outstretched hand, her feet dragging in the dirt.

"Please! Save me," she cried out.

"Get her, Jason. If he drains her now, he'll gain more strength. We'll deal with her later," Trin sent.

Jason broke from the group and grabbed Ann, while the girls worked to reinforce the shield. Heinrich was stuck behind the invisible wall, once again unable to move.

"You will not escape your fate this night," Trin threatened.

Kennedy, sprinkle the sulfur and salt at our feet. Trin spoke into her sister's mind.

An insidious sneer marred the demon's face as he tossed back his hood. "You think you can best me without your full powers? Tsk, tsk, tsk...how mistaken you are."

Another shockwave exploded through the cave, shattering Trin's shield into a million pieces. Finally reaching his altar, Heinrich thrust his hand into its center, piercing the petrified wood as if it was liquid. The small scythe he pulled out was ancient and hummed with power. This was the source of his magic.

He wasted no time in slashing his palm, dripping dark red blood into the cauldron. Trin worked silently to align the final pieces of her spell as they all watched his foul potion bubble and hiss.

They only needed a few more minutes for their full powers to return. The magical energy coursing through Trin's veins was unlike anything she had imagined. But as she stated before, it wasn't as simple as being in the same room, they could have done that weeks ago. No, there was much more to this spell than that, and she hoped her sisters didn't hate her for what she had to do.

Chapter Thirty-Three

"How did you and I become connected? My spell was cast only to save my sisters," Trin asked, trying to keep him talking.

Heinrich laughed. "You think the pups your mother spawned are your only sisters? How narrow-minded."

Trin stood silent, happy to take a tongue-lashing if it wasted more time.

"All true witches are your sisters, girl. That's why your spell pulled every last one of them from my time and into the future." Heinrich riffled through the folds of his cloak as he continued. "I couldn't let you rip my only means of survival from the world, so at the apex of your spell, I bound my soul to yours and followed you through time." His cocky sneer had

Trin wanting to burn him where he stood.

"If that's the case, then how did you become bound to this cave while Ann continued to roam free?" Caris asked.

Mocking turned to anger as the demon spat, "Like they say...all magic has a price."

Trin watched closely as Heinrich pulled a satchel from a hidden pocket within his robe.

"Ann was bound to me long before you cast your spell. But when I tethered myself to you, we were both fully fed from your magical energy. You are one powerful little witch." He licked his lips. "Only when I needed a boost to maintain the block I placed on you and your siblings, did Ann bring me a snack." He cackled then opened the satin bag, drawing out long strands of auburn hair.

This is why he hasn't attacked yet. Trin could feel, as could her sisters, that it was *her* hair the demon held. His intent was obvious as he dropped the strands into the cauldron. His goal was to reforge their connection; her flesh and his blood, mixing together as they both stood under the same roof, an opportunity he hadn't had in centuries.

Trin smirked as she felt the final piece of her spell snap into place. She looked at her sisters who both smiled, feeling their powers starting to rise.

At Trin's silent signal, Kennedy tossed a fireball from her fingertips, turning the hair in the demon's hand to ash, while

Caris dropped a spark at their feet, igniting the salt and sulfur which created an impassable barrier to all demon-kind.

"Times up," Trin proclaimed as she placed the pendant around her neck, grinning as the demon roared.

The energy between the sisters was now solid and whole, boosted by their mother's magic that had laid dormant, hidden deep within the pendant for centuries. All traces of the demon's red signature had been removed by the Goddess's hidden work just in time. The girls linked hands and gasped when a rush of pure magic flowed through them as Trin began her spell.

"Change in me, reflected be, as the Goddess's love washes over thee. Under the glow of this moon, we welcome the challenge of all that's new. Joy and pain, both a part, embraced with strength as this new chapter starts. Change in me, reflected be, as the Goddess's love washes over thee."

A whirlwind of smoke and sand, fire and air, all swarmed around them, separating them not only from the demon, but from the physical world.

The history of their family line flowed through them, continuing back to the root of magic itself. At its core, the Goddess stood waiting.

"You are now the most powerful of all my children, go forth and heal the world."

Transformation was inevitable when you ascend, but the outcome was far beyond anything Trin had imagined.

Empowered and fully in control, Trin opened her eyes to see Kara and Kenna as they once were, and knew she too was her old self.

"Karina," whispered Jason, who once again wore Jeremiah's face.

Trin smiled, knowing the next few minutes were only a blip on the wonderful new life that was being laid before them.

"You may have been a powerful demon once, corrupting witches spells and harnessing their magic, but the time has come for your race to end," Trin stated with an eerie calmness.

Heinrich laughed, unable to process the full extent of their powers. "You may have changed faces again, but you don't scare me little girl. Did you not think I would protect what's mine?"

Trin scoffed internally as she read his mind, then gazed at the walls and ceiling of the cave. With a mere thought, she summoned the demon's tooth Caris had obtained from Lillian into the palm of her hand.

Opening her mouth, Trin's voice rang loud and clear, creating the sound of tingsha chimes that vibrated and shook the entire cave.

The demon screamed, covering his ears, as the piercing sound shattered his protective net. A fine gray dust fell to the ground when Trin closed her fist, destroying the tooth.

"Your connection to this cave, to me, and to Ann has been

severed. You are no more," Trin proclaimed, evenly.

The level of power she and her sisters now possessed was beyond measure and knew no limit in this world or any other. With a flick of each of their wrists, the demon was destroyed— disintegrated before their very eyes.

With a swipe of her hand, Trin snuffed out the remaining barrier that burnt at their feet and walked towards Jason.

"What shall we do with her?" Jason asked, nodding to Ann who was still crouched at his feet.

The sisters looked at each other, and with an unspoken understanding, moved to encircle the lost witch.

"Ann Putnam, your bargain is done, and your life is again your own. The punishment for your deeds will be the stripping of your power, forcing you to live your remaining years as a mortal," Trin declared.

Ann stared at Trin, awe-struck and humbled as the magic flowed through her, removing even the tiniest spark of power. "I don't know what to do. I've been with you for so long."

Trin smiled, remembering the good times she had shared with Kit. "Try to make amends." With a snap of her fingers, Trin transported Ann to Salem, where she hoped the witch would start anew.

Jason reached for Trin, brushing a hand down her arm and smiled as visible blue energy flowed like a river between them. "It's over?"

"Yes and no," Trin said as she led them from the cave.

Jason and the girls gasped as they exited into the night.

There in the forest stood hundreds of witches.

"Welcome, my sisters and brothers. Our energy here tonight is what drew you to us, and now that our full powers are returned, we are to hide no more."

Trin raised her arms into the air. "Power heals and power binds, sending its call throughout time. Divided no more, united are we, the Witches of BlackBrook, forever the three."

Epilogue

The coven of witches cheered as Trin's spell washed over the crowd, unlocking their powers.

Some vanished with a pop, but others remained in the forest, celebrating the return of their heritage under the starry night. Fires glowed and songs rang out as the witches of old acknowledged Trin as their new High Priestess.

A man approached Trin, tapping her on the shoulder.

"My lady."

Trin gasped. It was the man from her stoop.

"Forgive me?" he begged with a smile. "I came to your door with a false story, wanting only to see the witch whose magic was calling to my blood. I had felt your presence for months, but only recently was I able to pinpoint your location. I hope I didn't offend."

Trin worked out the timeline in her mind. Once Kennedy had returned, their powers as the three must have been like a beacon to all the witches in the vicinity.

"I'm not offended at all," Trin replied. "Merry meet."

"And to you, merry meet," the gentleman replied, bowing before taking his leave.

"Are you ready for all this?" Jason whispered in her ear.

"Yes. I could feel them amassing while we were in the cave. Just like my spell before, our energy drew them here. I'm honored they chose me."

"There could be no one else," Jason kissed her hand, acknowledging her new position.

Trin found Caris and Kennedy dancing around the fire.

"Are you upset with me?" she asked in a rush, tossing her worries to the flame.

"For what?" Caris begged.

"For changing us back and creating this community for us to maintain?" Trin confessed.

Caris and Kennedy looked at each other, seeing the faces they were both born with and tackled Trin with a hug.

"Sister...you've freed us," Caris said. "Together we will use our magic to heal this world as the Goddess instructed, one fight at a time with the help of our fellow witches."

Jason joined them and asked the obvious question, "But how are we to return to our lives, now that everything has changed so much?"

"Seamlessly," Trin replied. "Our lives are still our own, and everyone we've ever known will see us as we've always been. There will be no confusion for the mortals."

Jason gathered Trin into his arms and placed a kiss upon her lips. "You've thought of everything."

Trin looked at her sisters and beamed. "Not quite everything. I think we need to reevaluate our living arrangements. With our powers returned we are stronger together and with an active coven, we'll be conducting rituals and holding Sabbaths on a regular basis."

The girls laughed and yanked Trin and Jason into a group hug. With a snap of her fingers Caris transported them and the truck all back to the house.

"Welcome home, Trin." Caris smiled.

"You mean it?"

"Of course! You said it yourself, we're the Witches of BlackBrook. This is where we belong."

The End

About the Author

Award Winning Author, Tish Thawer, writes paranormal romances for all ages. From her first paranormal cartoon, Isis, to the Twilight phenomenon, myth, magic, and superpowers have always held a special place in her heart.

Tish is known for her detailed world-building and magic-laced stories. Her work has been compared to Nora Roberts, Sam Cheever, and Charlaine Harris. She has received nominations for a RONE Award (Reward of Novel Excellence), and Author of the Year (Fantasy, Dystopian, Mystery), as well as nominations and wins for Best Cover, and Reader's Choice Award.

Tish has worked as a computer consultant, photographer, and graphic designer, and is a columnist for Gliterary Girl media and has bylines in RT Magazine and Literary Lunes Magazine. She resides in Colorado with her husband and three wonderful children and is represented by Gandolfo, Helin, and Fountain Literary Management.

You can find out more about Tish and her all titles by visiting: www.TishThawer.com

And don't forget to follow her on Facebook for all the latest news: www.facebook.com/AuthorTishThawer

Ready for another adventure?
Turn the page for an excerpt from *DARK ABIGAIL*,
Book 2 in The Women of Purgatory Trilogy.

Excerpt

by

Tish Thawer

I surveyed the death and destruction surrounding me and smiled. Another job well done. The fog and spindly trees that accompanied my arrival began to recede, returning the surroundings back to their normal state. It was something I never tired of; something that fed into my legend and mystique. For I am Dark Abigail—Hell's first assassin.

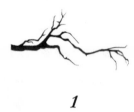

1

Loki peered through a rip in space, his nostrils flaring at his recent failure. He forced himself to watch as Raven and Michael bid farewell to Holli and Garrett in a slew of hugs and kisses.

"Holli and Garrett," he snarled. His daughter would pay for her betrayal and the new leader of Purgatory would lose his head in the process. Angered by the choice she had made, the sight of her embracing her new life with Death was too much to bear.

Loki turned away and focused his full attention on his current surroundings. A black expanse of lava cooled fields stretched out before him. Blood red rivers of molten fire flowed throughout, illuminating the tips and crevices, creating a sea of eerie shapes and a sense of false movement.

Traipsing through Hell with diminished powers wasn't going to be easy, but he had a plan to put into action, and keeping Lucifer waiting was never a good idea.

His first step towards Lucifer's castle conjured images of Thor, Odin, and Frigga—specters of his worst memories: fear, anger, and guilt. They swarmed around him like vengeful ghosts, but it was to be expected...this was Hell after all.

Still want more?
Turn the page for an excerpt from
HANDLER, Tish Thawer's upcoming New
Adult Dystopian.

Excerpt

Handler

by

Tish Thawer

P.R.O.L.O.G.U.E.

"Don't do it, Cole," Samantha whispered as we crouched behind the wall.

The thick cover of night limited my vision, but I didn't have to see her face to know she was about to cry.

"Sam, I'll be fine. I'm just going to run over and make sure Kiva and Vey made it across the bridge."

"Who cares!" She sobbed. "They're the reason we're breaking the law in the first place. It would serve them right."

I shifted my position and laid a hand on her knee. "You don't mean that. Kiva is your friend, and Vey is only searching for his brother. They aren't trying to get us in trouble. Besides, you didn't have to come."

She jerked at the harshness of my words, but it was true. None of us *twisted her arm or forced her to tag along.*

"You don't get it, do you? I'm not worried about getting in trouble, I'm worried that we're all going to die! You know the stories, Cole; you know we're forbidden to go out at night."

. . . . . .

"Cole! You ready?" Ren's shout pulled me from the memory of that fateful day.

"Yeah, let's do this."

I glanced at the tape covering my hands and pushed the padding between each knuckle. Since I'd been *accepted* into the Handler program, my fights had become harder and harder and the damage to my body more and more apparent. Tonight's fight determined whether I'd remain in my current job, or if I'd advance and have a chance to be placed in a government position.

I looked down the long dark corridor at the illuminated stairs and imagined the waiting crowd beyond.

My stomach rolled.

I shook my head and punched each fist into the opposite hand, psyching myself up. *You've got this!*

Actually, there was no choice, I had to win; I *had* to get placed in the government if I ever hoped to expose their lie. Even if it meant moving onto the killing rounds.

C.H.A.P.T.E.R. O.N.E.

May 2069...

"Colizan, would you care to join us for a walk?" Father asked.

I looked up from my history book and smiled. "Of course, it would be my pleasure."

The warm sun glinted off the quartz sidewalk as my father, mother, and I strolled from our assigned dwinn in the Northern territory of Atal. Winding our way through the gardens which led to Common Park had always been their preferred route. Picture perfect displays of green grass, sparking quartz, lush flowers, and elaborate water features dotted the landscape. Mother and Father chatted enthusiastically just ahead of me, but I didn't bother eavesdropping on their conversation. Instead, I continued to take in the scenery I'd enjoyed for all of my eighteen years. I tilted my head back and appreciated the glass and quartz buildings that lined the sky. Some were tall and towering, others round and inviting, and I loved them all. I sighed and quickened my pace as we approached my favorite part of the city—the museum. It reminded me of a picture I'd once seen of the Sydney Opera House in Australia, but instead of white and cream concrete, it was all glass. Ever since I was young, I always made it a point to stop and read the plaque outside, and today was no exception.

"ATAL. Est. 2027. Redesigned from the ashes of Atlanta." An image of a Genesis machine hovered over the war-struck city in the foreground, and in the background stood the utopian paradise it left in its wake. The large spaceship-like device with its metallic domed body and long tendrils of machinery hanging down had always amazed me.

"I didn't know there was a meeting today," Father stated, pulling my attention from the sign.

I glanced up and found folks gathered in Common Park, taking seats on the bleachers that had automatically risen from the grass.

"Let's find a seat," Mother suggested.

We ventured into the park, nodding our greetings to the other citizens, including Merta, one of our neighbors.

"What's this about, Cecily?" Merta asked my mother.

"I'm not sure," Mom replied, sliding her thin frame into a seat.

Father guided me into the bleachers, claiming the outer seat for himself. The action seemed odd and somewhat defensive, as if he was preparing in case we needed to make a sudden exit.

"What's wrong?" I whispered as the rest of the citizens filed into place.

"I don't know," Dad replied.

"Welcome!" A hidden voice boomed over the crowd. "We've requested your presence here today for an important announcement," an Official declared.

My mother leaned across me and whispered to my father, "We must have missed the announcement while on our walk. But why wouldn't they just send a message to the com-link in our dwinn?"

My father's reply was clipped and wordless. However, the rise of his eyebrow and quick shrug of his muscular shoulder spoke volumes.

"It's with heavy hearts we inform you that one of our citizens has disappeared and is presumed dead." A large holographic image of my friend, Viktor Fenton, appeared in front of the crowd. Mother gasped and covered her mouth, mirroring the collective response.

"This is the third disappearance within the last six months. Therefore, we've called this meeting to remind you of our one and only law. A law that is in place for *your* safety. Please heed our warning and do not go out at night. If you violate the law, these are the kind of terrible things that will continue to happen, and we cannot bear to lose any more citizens of our beloved Atal." Viktor's blonde-haired image brightened and began rotating in midair.

I squirmed in my seat, not because my long legs or broad

shoulders felt confined in this tiny space, but because their attempt at trying to make us feel as if they cared wasn't working. Atal had plenty of rules to keep our lives structured from day-to-day, but only one law; *Don't go out at night.* My family had never broken the law or any of the rules—well, besides me I supposed. In my early teenage years, before I'd gone through Ancient Holographic Studies in school, I'd hacked some old movies and books to feed my curiosity about the world before the war. However, it was in those times when my curiosity peaked, that my father would remind me, *"It's the rules that allow us to live in peace and harmony, and therefore we should be grateful for them."* So, all in all, we were the appropriate family clan. But as I looked at my father now, his strained muscles, furrowed brow, and tight jaw made it obvious that something strange was happening here—that something was off about this impromptu meeting and the message being delivered.

"Let's go," Father snapped. We quickly rose from our seats, Mother pausing to gaze at Viktor's image one last time.

Reaching our dwinn, Father placed the palm of his hand against the security panel and the thick opaque door opened in a smooth rush. "Okay, now will you tell me what's going on?" I inquired the moment we were inside.

"No."

"Why?"

"Because I don't know," he stated flatly.

My jaw flexed, and I gritted my teeth as he turned away.

"Cecily, please contact Lyree and pay our respects," Father instructed.

"Of course."

The three of us gathered around the video com-link in the kitchen and waited for my mother to dial the extension for the Fenton family dwinn.

"Cecily..." sobbed Viktor's mother. "It can't be true. My Viktor would never go out after dark. Never!" Lyree's discarded tears coated her cheeks.

"Lyree, please accept our sincerest condolences," Father stated politely.

I hung my head and stared at my hands while my parents continued to listen to Viktor's mother. Their efforts to console her were merely a lesson in futility.

I looked up when there was a break in the conversation and flinched. Vey, Viktor's twin brother, was barely visible in the far back corner of the screen and staring straight at me. I opened my mouth, ready to pay my own respect, but stopped short when he jerked his blonde head to the side and disappeared from view. I quietly excused myself and made my way to the com-link in my private room.

I pressed the *accept* button on the screen and found Vey waiting on the display.

"I'm so sorry, man." My words fell short of the feelings

behind them.

"Thanks."

"Any clue what really happened?" I asked.

"No. A bunch of us were walking back from the Education Center yesterday, and one minute he was there and the next he wasn't." Vey sank onto his bed. "Only when I turned around to ask him a question did I realize he was gone. We backtracked as far as we could, looking for...well, anything, but once the night alarms began to sound, we all rushed home. I immediately told my mother what happened, and she submitted an emergency report right away."

"Was there an investigation? Did the Officials figure out what happened?"

"No. We got the same report as everyone else, only they told us in private instead of in the park. Their 'official' statement is that it looks like he decided to split from our group and venture into the night on his own, which led to his probable death."

Vey raised his head, staring into the display. The piercing determination behind his green eyes told me everything I needed to know. He wasn't buying their story and we were going to investigate on our own.

I didn't bother arguing because I couldn't agree more. Vey wouldn't have broken the law...but we were about to. "When do we start looking?"

"Tomorrow night. Kiva's coming too."

"Okay. I'll check with Sienna and we can confirm our plans tomorrow at school." I reached for the *end* button but paused when Vey said my name.

"Cole?" I turned back to the display and found Vey's gratitude shining in his eyes. "Thank you. You're a true friend."